Smithland

Written by Kyle Dorsey, copyright ©Kyle Dorsey 2013

D1521708

The following is a compilation of chilling events staged in a town deep within the Pine Barons known as "Smithland". Each character will tell their own tales, speak their own words, and reveal darkness the likes of which may shock you to the very bone. If you feel compelled, you may continue reading, but remember, you've been warned.

Bob the Butcher

Recently, my girlfriend Brooklyn and I, decided to move into our first house. It was a small house with one bedroom and one bathroom, but for our first house, it would suffice. The neighborhood we moved to was far off from the city we both grew up in. We both had this strong interest for nature and travel, so we moved to a town called Smithland, a small town buried in the Pine Barons of New Jersey. The residents of this small town seem friendly, but are very quiet and keep to themselves. Even the real estate woman (whom you would expect to be bubbly and cheerful) was extremely quiet, as she almost had this look of fear on her face. We decided to pass it off and assumed that she was just a shy person.

After about a month, we had finally settled in and began restoration on the house. We mainly did yard work, being that we didn't really have the money for any major restorations. One day, while cleaning

3

weeds out of the garden, I happened upon a manhole cover. I found this a bit strange, considering the location of the house. It seemed like there should be no access to the sewer from here. Curious, I retrieved a crowbar from the shed and pried open the cover. I peered inside, only to find total darkness and a few rungs at the beginning of a ladder. I continued down, my interest peaked at the thought of what I might find. I felt my foot hit the ground as I reached the end of the ladder. I fumbled through my pockets for a lighter, flicked the top, and began inspecting the room. Each wall was decorated with a vast assortment of knives. In the middle of the room sat a desk with a sharpener and a clown mask seated on top.

The mask was different from other masks I'd seen in many ways. The texture had me curious as to what it might be made out of. To hold the mask in place, two leather straps ran along the back and connected to the sides. I placed the mask back onto the desk, and continued my inspection. At the side of the desk sat a large box which was covered in dust. I swiped the dust away with my fingertips, and drew the flaps away from the box. Inside, I found an old film projector and one reel of film. I thought to myself, what kind of past this house might have, and what clues the film might provide and decided to retrieve it with me into the house.

I drew the shades and dimmed the lights, then started the projector and began the film. The film was grainy, but based on the attire and apparel of the people in the film, this must have been recorded around the 90's. It appeared to be a child's birthday. In the film, a man and a woman were shown smiling and holding each other while watching as, who I could only assume were their child and friends, were being entertained by a clown. The makeup the clown wore had strikingly similar designs to the mask I had found. The film cut out and I began to rise from my chair. Suddenly and unexpectedly, the film re-collected and continued on. In this part of the film, only the woman was shown. She didn't smile this time. She only stared blankly as her son, and what appeared to be only half of the children from the original section of the film, were entertained by the same clown. Suddenly, the group turned toward the camera, staring at something behind it with looks of fear and loathing. A man stepped on camera who had similar characteristics to the man in the first film, but still different. This time, darkness and evil radiated off of him. His muscles were toned in an almost sickly manner. I watched as the children ran over to the mother as he screamed and shouted at the group, I could see the mother weep and mouth what appeared to be, "ROBERT! NO!". This appeared to faze him in an almost terrifying manner. He screamed and flipped a table, almost flinging it across the yard. Next, he approached the clown, grabbing him by the throat and flinging him down to the ground. He removed a marker from his pocket, and then started drawing lines along the outer parts of his face. Then, he removed a sharp knife from his pocket, slowly and steadily, began cutting through the flesh like paper. I wondered what I found more disturbing, the act, or how precise his cuts were. The man stopped. He rose slowly and turned around. I vomited as I saw his face, for now I knew what the mask I had found was made from. The man stood facing the group, the clown's face stretched over his, like a mask. He gazed for a few moments at them with a sadistic look in his eyes.

Bob, I've decided to call him Bob, marked his final atrocious act in the film by drawing a hand gun from his waist, then shot each of the guests dead, one by one. I vomited once more as the film cut out. I was shocked not only by what I had seen, but what had happened in my own back yard. I decided not to tell Brooklyn. I couldn't corrupt this house for her, as the film had for me.

Hours had passed, and the visions of what I had seen had still not left my mind. I had finished my work and gone to bed, completely restless. Brooklyn returned home and found me awake. She had been putting in extra hours at work, which had caused her to return later at night.

"Why are you still awake, hon?" She asked, confused. All that I could do is kiss her head as she crawled into bed with me, and pray that holding my love in my arms would comfort me.

It was 3:00 a.m. I hadn't slept at all. Brooklyn was sound asleep. God, how I envied her. I rose out of bed and looked out the window. Raindrops were heavily falling and lightning flashed across the sky. A storm had rolled in about a half an hour ago. I walked to the window and watched the raindrops fall, as they splashed against the concrete streets in waves. I felt myself finally relaxing as I listened to the sound of the rain patter against the window. I let my eyes sink at the thought that I might finally get some rest tonight.

My heart stopped as my eyes reached street level. There, on the other side of the street, stood the dark figure of a man looking back at me. I couldn't see his face, but I knew it was him, by that same chill he gave me when I saw the film. I stared for what felt like hours, until I saw him draw something sliver from his waist. I squinted to get a better look. It was a gun. Before I had time to react, I heard the loud bang followed by an echo, and I saw the flash in the chamber of the gun. I winced, waiting for the bullet to make impact, although it never did. It was a blank. He was toying with me. I looked back at the street, only to find that he was gone. I crawled into bed and wrapped my arms around Brooklyn, fearful for both of our lives.

The next morning I woke up to the sound of Brooklyn cooking breakfast in the kitchen. I looked at the clock. It was 8:00 a.m. I hadn't fallen asleep until 5:00 a.m. I'd have to go through the day on only three hours of rest. I drug myself out of bed and stumbled down the hallway, still trying to wake up. I made it to the kitchen, where I sat down, hazily rubbed the sleep from my eyes, and tried to greet Brooklyn with a smile. Her face remained emotionless.

Concern radiated from her as she made her way around the kitchen. She scraped the eggs she had been cooking onto my plate, then sat down next to me, staring at me with a stern, yet worrisome expression.

"What happened last night, David?", she asked with a choke in her voice.

"What do you mean?", I asked as innocently as I could.

"You were still awake when I got home. You were pale as a ghost. You hardly slept. You looked terrified, you still do."

Her eyes watered as she spoke. She was pained. I felt guilty keeping such a dark secret from such a sweet girl.

"It's nothing. I'm just not settled in yet. All of the new people, the new sights, this house. I'll be okay, I promise."

I prayed that she wouldn't see through my lie. I couldn't have her as terrified as I am, not after she's been so happy since we moved here.

"Okay. If you need to talk, you know I'm always here, babe." She pressed her soft lips against my cheek, then walked away. I sighed, both in relief and discontent with how I couldn't convince myself to tell her what I knew.

I finished my breakfast, and went to the yard to continue restoration on the house while Brooklyn left for work. I spent the entire day drowning in paranoia, always watching over my shoulder, knowing he was somewhere nearby. I'd watch carefully as I'd mowed the lawn, raked the leaves, and continued removing weeds from the yard, wondering where he could be hiding. I spent hours working out in the hot sun. As soon as I'd finish one project, I'd start on the next. I needed anything that could keep me active and alert with a good eye on my surroundings, that way, no matter what his next move was, I'd at least see him coming. By the time Brooklyn had returned home, I was exhausted. My arms, neck, and face were beat red and burnt from the sun. I could hardly walk. She helped me to the bedroom, and we both went to bed. I laid awake waiting for her to fall asleep, waiting for a chance to go back to guard duty to see if I could scope out Bob the Butcher. My nights work turned up fruitless, and I spent the next few days with the same routine. I'd get between two and three hours of sleep each night after keeping watch.

I took his lack of activity as a sign that he was gone. I thought to myself, "If he wanted to harm us, he would have surely done it by now." After the first couple of days, I started feeling the toll my paranoia had put on my mind. I had begun losing touch with the world around me, and nothing made sense anymore. I heard voices that came from nowhere, I saw shadows that weren't there. I needed to see a doctor, but had convinced myself that I just needed rest.

It had been two weeks with no sign of Bob the Butcher. I had made a full recovery, and I could finally hold Brooklyn and feel comfort again. One night, after finishing my hard work, I decided to relax with some TV. Brooklyn was at work, so I was home alone again. The show I was watching was some documentary about "The world's worst serial killers". I thought to myself, "They can't even compare to Bob!" laughing to myself, feeling that it was all behind me. I also thought to myself about whether or not the history of our house, was the reason so many of our neighbors had kept to themselves.

I looked out the window. Lightning flashed across the sky and thunder shook the house, then, I heard the loud click as the power cut out. Before my encounter, I used to always enjoy storms like this. I did my best to remain calm, but a thought grew in my mind that reminded me that if he was still here, without television, without radio, without anything to distract me, it would just be he and I. I rushed to the front door and locked it, though this was not enough to make me feel secure. I hurried to the kitchen to grab the biggest knife I could find, and then sat tensely at the kitchen table. I sat for hours, the storm not dying down, and I had fallen asleep. My eyes creaked open about four hours later and I looked at the clock.

11:53 p.m. Brooklyn should have been home by now.

Before I had the chance to rise up from the table to see if she was home, I heard a sound that made my heart race, and sent a chill down my spine. It was the sound of something sharp and metallic being driven across the side of the house, almost as if someone was cutting it with a knife. It ran the course of the house, beginning from the back, and tracing to the front door, where it stopped. For at least thirty seconds, there was dead silence. Then, there were three slow, light knocks. I rose up from the table slowly, bracing the knife in my hand for attack. The knocks repeated, growing louder each time, as if whoever was on the other side of the door was losing their patience. There was one final loud thud, then a crash. Whoever was there, broke through the door.

Heavy footsteps echoed down the hallway, approaching the kitchen. Terrified, I ran around the house, looking for another outlet, scurrying about like a trapped rat. I dashed through the doorway to the living room, only to be struck abruptly by a heavy, brick-like fist, large enough to make an impact from the top of my skull, to the tip of my chin. I fell back in a daze, and looked up at my attacker. Lightning flashed, revealing his painted, grinning face. He wore a ragged tank top, old, worn jeans, the clown mask from the bunker, and the same twisted look he had in the film. In his hand, he held a disembodied head, which was still dripping with blood. Whose, I could not tell. Or at least, not until he rolled it to me. He swung one arm up, flinging the head towards me lightly, sending it bouncing, then rolling to my side. It stopped with the eyes staring directly into mine. It was Brooklyn. She held a disturbed, pained look on her face. The same she may have held in her passing. I choked, nearly starting to cry at the sight of my lost love, then looked back at him.

He stood there, looking into my eyes with a vulgar presence of evil, and finally spoke with a thick, gravelly voice. "You should have told her."

He was right. If I had only told her, she might still be alive. It had been MY fault. Before I could have a second thought, he kicked me flat to the ground, stepping on my chest so that I couldn't move. He leaned in close to my face, breathing heavily, then with a chilling voice, spoke. "You were the lucky one. You knew that I was coming for you. Next time, you won't be as fortunate."

He took the same knife that I had seen in the film from a holster that was strapped to his waist, then, grabbed me tightly by the throat, strangling me and forcing my tongue out of my mouth. With one clean swipe by the blade, my tongue flew from my mouth, then flopped to the ground. Blood oozed out like a waterfall, and I screamed at the intense pain that I felt. He leaned in close again,

"You won't be able to yell for help", he said, then threw the knife to the side.

Next, he drew out two smaller flat handled knives, which he placed between his fingers as he made a fist. He struck my face with the force of a speeding car, the blades piercing my eyes.

"You won't be able to see me coming", I could hear him say.

I choked on my own blood, vomiting back up the amount that I had swallowed. I couldn't see, but I knew he was still there. He leaned forward; I could feel his breath circulating throughout my ear.

"You won't be able to hear me coming." he said, before jamming what felt like two metal rods into my ears, rupturing both of my ear drums.

I laid there, praying that he would finish me off, only to feel my discontent as I felt the vibrations of his footsteps going from heavy, to light. He was leaving. I groaned, knowing that my pain was not over. Now, I lay here, in a puddle of my own blood. I can hardly move... but I tell myself, "If I can just find Brooklyn's body, I can fix her!"

I stumble, trying to balance myself as I pull up off the floor....All that I need to do is find her body....I can fix her....Things will be normal again....I will HOLD her AGAIN!

The Wanderer

I have no idea what time it is. I've been laying here, in a pool of my own blood for what seems like hours. My Brooklyn is out there some where. I can find her, and I can fix her. I jutted my head back and forth, side to side, praying that at least one of my senses would return. Vision, no. Hearing, no. I tried to curse, but all that I could produce were harsh, guttural sounds. I began dragging myself through the house. I'd have to at least find my way to the street, if I was going to get help.

I'd use touch to find my path. When I had reached the couch in the living room, I knew I was close. I continued dragging myself until I reached the door. An intense amount of pain shot through my body like electricity as I rose up off the ground, if only long enough to pop open the door. I immediately collapsed to the ground, then began dragging myself once more. As I reached the street, I had a painful revelation. The last time I had looked at the clock, had the ability to look at the clock, it was 2:30 in the morning. No one would be out on the streets this late at night. I groaned in pain, then did the only thing I could think of to save myself.

I picked myself up once more, limping down the sidewalk to the neighbors house. I collapsed once more on the door step of the house. The blood loss was taking it's toll. I tried working up the energy to knock, but could only push myself to jab my fingernails into the door, and begin clawing like a wounded animal. It was no use. With the hope that someone might be awake, I drug myself around to the back of the house, thinking that I might be seen through the window of the back door. Dragging myself up to the door, I began, once again, clawing. I clawed until I felt the warm ooze of blood gush out of skinless gaps, where my fingernails had broken off. I focused my energy and concentrated. If I lost three of my senses, maybe I could use what I had left to explore my surroundings. I could feel

20

vibrations that I had identified as a foot step behind me. I knew that behind the house sat the border of the woods, but waved this away with the thought that our neighbors might have been out for a late night walk. With what strength I could manage, I picked myself up, then weakly stumbled towards the footsteps. I had reached my destination, and with a pained gasp, began mouthing the word "Help", hoping my savior would understand. Just then, I had the sensation of what felt like large branches striking me erupt from my ribs. I went down, and, having used the last of my energy, I passed out.

I woke up in a daze, still without sight our sound, but felt that I was being drug across the rugged terrain of the woods. The stinging sensation of twigs across my skin, and the feeling of leaves crackling underneath me let me know that I was alive. I thought about who my captor might be. One of the things that the local sheriff warned us about when we had moved in was the kind of people that would dwell in the woods at this time of night. Reports of satanists and cults were thick in this part of the state. I could feel the warmth of a fire. It was intense, almost as if I, myself, had been set ablaze. As I shuttered over the intensity of this feeling, I began to hear again. It was dull at first, but it grew. The first sound I heard was the sound of a large group of people chanting, similar to what you might expect from a coven of monks, only darker. The sound of chanting hummed in, growing louder. I'd have to estimate, but it sounded like there might have been between twelve and fifteen people.

Finally, my vision started returning. I woke up to the sight of several people dressed in long black robes, with medallions dangling from their necks, which glimmered by the light of the fire. They stood around the fire and I, chanting. I wondered where I was. "This must be a cult.", I thought to myself, observing how foreign the emblems on the medallions appeared to be. The chanting stopped, and it grew silent again. Three of the cloaked invaders stepped back, allowing what appeared to be a leader of the ceremony stepped in. He wore the same cloak as the rest of the group, but with a slightly different medallion. This one had snakes interlinking and tangling across the outside circle of the medallion, and an upside down star in the center of it all. Around his shoulders, he wore a clean, pressed, red sash. He marched up to me with a serious expression on his face. The kind you might expect a business man to wear. He stopped in front of me, peering down from the peak of his nose. His eyes were an unnatural shade of yellow that seemed to glow..

He spoke in a sophisticated manner, with a deep voice, "You needed help, Daniel." He held up my drivers license and began reading my information.

"You were lucky my children had found you."

"Wuuuhhhh". I struggled to form words, but I had to ask, I couldn't take the curiosity any longer.

"Where are we?". Even through my babbling, he could understand what I wanted to ask.

"You're in my home. My name is Ossiarus, executive to the dark throne. And you are Daniel Barger, weight: one hundred and eighty five pounds, black hair, eyes....WERE green." He paused and smirked to himself, seemingly laughing at his own crude joke, then continued, "You seem to be perfect for the little project that we have, Mr. Barger. But, because I am a man of business, I will reward you for your compliance if you agree."

I nodded, not wanting to force more garbled words and look a fool. "Tell me sir, what is it that your heart desires most?" He replied, a gleam ever present in his eyes. I didn't have to think of my reply, it's what I had sworn that I'd do the instant this madness began.

"Murrrhhhh, murrrh" I forced my words out once more, then pointed to my heart.

"Ah, yes. Brooklyn, your love interest. You lost her, didn't you? The stench of morn and loss arriarate off of you in the masses. We can bring her back for you, but she'll come once you fulfill your part of our agreement. You may have noticed that you can see and hear again. These are both, allowed to you to conduct our business, and your first payment for the project you're about to take on."

"Marlllaaahhhhrrr" I replied, asking what exactly this project had in store for me.

"Oh, you'll learn in due time. Right now, the important question is whether or not you'll be able to see Brooklyn again." He said as he pulled up his sleeve.

Carved along his arm were several signatures. Sarah, Jeremiah, Thomas, Alice, the list spread further, traveling up the dark area of his arm, shadowed by his sleeve. Along the side was an empty space, not yet touched. He held out a knife.

"Carve your signature, and we shall begin". I grabbed the knife, millions of thoughts flowing through my mind at once. "This will end badly!", "You don't know what you're getting yourself into!", "You're going to get yourself killed!", but one erupted over the others like thunder, "YOU WILL HOLD BROOKLYN AGAIN!"

I carved my signature, then looked back up at him. He smiled, as if he had felt no pain. "ALL WELCOME BROTHER BARGER!" He said, lifting me up above his head, clutching me by the chest.

The chanting resumed, as he bellowed out a deep laugh, then, with one quick movement, flung me into the fire. The pain was intense. I looked at my arms. The flesh began searing off like paper, exposing tendons and muscle, and then bone. I felt the flesh and muscle in my legs melt away the same way, as I fell back, no longer able to support myself, the midnight sky being the only thing that I could see before I blacked out.

I woke up at home, in my bed. It was still night. I sat up quick, then looked at my arms. Everything appeared to be fine, all flesh in place, but still a bit pale. I thought to myself, wondering whether or not I had dreamt everything that had happened that night, but the realism of every moment hammered away like a jack hammer. I stepped out of bed, feeling new life. I felt refreshed and strong again, but a bit dehydrated. I walked out of my bedroom and down the hall to the bathroom, marching with a new sense of strength. I stopped at the sink, peered down at the glass that was waiting next to the faucet for me, then looked back up and into the mirror above it. I almost fell back at the sight of what I felt had to be a nightmare. There, staring back at me through the mirror, was the reflection of some....beast. It had no eyes, but very dim blue lights in the middle of two empty eye sockets. It's jaw hung, broken, swaying like a swinging door in the wind. It's flesh was sheer white, like a corpse. This new, horrific monster that haunts my house was me. Reality came flowing in. Everything that had happened was painfully true. Bob the Butcher, the cult, the agreement with Ossairus to follow along with some mysterious project. It was all true. Brooklyn was gone, her head the only thing I have left.....HER HEAD!

I ran to the living room, to where I could remember Brooklyn's head rolling like a ball to my side. It was still there. Her eyes still as beautiful as always, and her long black hair, flowing out naturally. Her lips seemed to carry a sense of both lifelessness and being at the same time. Her skin soft to the touch, but a grey faded color. She had began to rot. "I must preserve her!" I thought to myself, cradling her in my arms like one would a child. I rummaged through the kitchen, flinging around pots and pans, smashing plates as I threw them aside, looking for a large jar. At last, I had found one. I scooped up Brooklyn's head, then gently placed it inside. Next, I would need some embalming fluid to prevent her from rotting any further. I stopped in my tracks before leaving. I couldn't be seen around town with this appearance. They'd think I was a monster. I darted to the garage, then started throwing boxes aside, looking for the marker-streaked "Halloween" label. Finally, finding the box I was looking for, I threw open the flaps then dug for my mask. It was a plain white theater mask, nothing outrageous, and nothing that would attract too much attention. I slid it on, feeling the elastic band snap against the back of my head, sinking into my cold, dead flesh, then set out on foot, on my way to the Smithland Funeral Home.

I arrived around mid-afternoon and the sun had already begun to set, peaking just barely behind the trees. I approached the front doors of the funeral home, spotting the hearse in the driveway. The mortician was in. I'd have to be strategic with my movements in order to get in, get the embalming fluid, then leave undetected. I slowly opened the door, watching between the crack as it slowly creaked open to make sure that I was alone. The interior was dimly lit, save the sunlight passing through the windows that bordered the room. No one there. In one smooth movement I slipped in and closed the door behind me, then ventured down the hallway that awaited me. The door at the end of the hall had been left open, revealing stairs down to the basement. "This is where they'd keep the embalming fluid", I thought to myself ask I slowly crept down the stairs. I gazed around the room, almost in awe. I had never seen so many jars, vials, and mortuary tools in my life. It felt like being in a museum of decay. It was something that, before my incident I had no interest in, but recently, have developed a deep love for. Suddenly, I heard the heavy, quick footsteps of someone coming down the stairs. My mind tried, desperately begging me to hide, but to no avail. It was drowned out by a burning sensation that began to rise up in my chest. It was dark, fiery, and strangely comforting. A sick grin crept across my elongated face as I grabbed the closest knife I could find, then waited for the mortician to arrive, unknowingly walking into his dark demise.

I ducked down behind the table in the center of the room, thinking what fun it would be reaping the poor old man of his existence. He walked across the room, completely unaware of my presence, then began inspecting the jars on the counter at the end of the room. I could feel my grin growing wider, and I felt as though the skin along the corners of my mouth would rip, and as I snuck up behind him, a cool chill shot down my spine that gave me a lustful feeling. In a flash, the palm of my hand covered his face, a muffled "HELP!" leaked out, and at that instant, the blade swam across the flesh of his neck like a fish. He dropped to the floor. Unexpectedly, I found myself bombarded with an odd sense of dizziness. I looked down at my victim, first with shock, then, of acceptance. Is this the business agreement I had reached with Ossiarus starting to take effect? Before last night, I would have never considered an act like this... But then again, do I really care? I watched the blood drip from the knife in a steady stream, and watched the blood pool around the mortician's body. "What a beautiful chain of events." I said to myself, squatting, then dipping my fingers into the blood.

The warmth gave me an intense feeling of satisfaction. I loved what I had done, every bit of it. I wanted more, killing him wasn't enough. With my palms cupped, I scooped up a puddle of blood, and began drinking. "Delicious", I whispered to myself. Compelled, I removed my mask, plunged face first into the puddle, and began slurping wildly like a dog, until none remained. I plopped back, my back against the counter, and sighed. This would become my new hobby. This is how I would spend the rest of my days on this earth, killing, filling my gullet with the blood and flesh of my victims, then collecting whatever trophy I could. The only thing that could glorify this moment, is ending it with the embrace of my dear, sweet Brooklyn. I stood up, sorted through the jars until I found my embalming fluid, then retreated from the house, enjoying the sensation of satisfaction coarsening through my veins. I navigated my surroundings, looking for a garage. I'd need a vehicle.

Something with enough room for the mortician's corpse. He was a portly man.

I didn't have the strength to carry him far enough to hide the body. I could take his car, but a new hearse parked in my driveway wasn't exactly inconspicuous. Neighboring the house was an old shed, the doors cracked open. I opened them the rest of the way to find an old Model AA Ford truck. The truck was worn. The body rusted, the windshield cracked, and the wooden fencing surrounding the bed of the truck was rotted. I reached between the hood and the grill of the truck, grabbing the lever that rests within, then pulled. The hood popped open, awaiting inspection. The engine glimmered in the light, seemingly proudly puffing it's chest out to show that it was new, along with many other parts. Whoever this truck belonged to had clearly been working on restoring it. The situation seemed promising, so I slammed the hood shut, slid into the driver's seat of the old machine, and reached for the keys, which were resting on the dashboard. I cranked the ignition only twice. The engine roared, the cab shook, and the exhaust sputtered, bringing this old, rotting creature to life. It was perfect. Well, maybe not perfect. It still wasn't the most conspicuous vehicle I could find, but I loved it. It almost seemed to live and breathe like a rabid animal. Like my pet. I left the engine running as I climbed out of the driver's seat and retrieved the mortician's body to the truck. I heaved his colossal body onto the bed of the truck using all of my strength, then collected a tarp from the garage to hide the corpse. Next, I slid into the cab of my new pet, shifted into gear, and heard the loud roar as the great beast began rolling forward.

The drive home was comforting. I took the main road through town, watching it's citizens shuffle down the sidewalks and through the streets. I scoped them out, thinking of who I might take as my next victim. I was new to this game, and I imagined that each kill would bring me a different kind of thrill. Should I kill a woman? Another man? Maybe a child... Maybe a doctor... Maybe a lawyer. The possibilities were endless. The truck rolled to a stop as I entered the driveway of my house. I stepped out, then took a few deep breathes before heaving armfuls of human lard connected to a poorly out of shape torso from the bed of the truck. I drug the corpse into the garage, leaving him to rot under a large pile of boxes, garbage, and debris that had already been scattered throughout the room.

Next, I retrieved the jar of embalming fluid from the cab of the truck and entered the house. "HONEY, I'M HOME!" I shouted, grinning at my horribly cliché entrance. I approached the kitchen table, where I had left Brooklyn's head, then picked it up once more, once again, admiring hear beautiful, long black hair, her light blue eyes, and her delicate lips. She was almost as beautiful as she was the day we first met, save the missing torso. I held her close to my face, then softly pressed my lips passionately against her dead, frozen lips. I held her like this for long, not wanting to let go. I inserted my tongue between the loosely closed lips, and flicked hers, then began massaging it gently. The inside of her mouth was dry, not having produced saliva in roughly a day and a half, but oh, how I enjoyed it. I paused, then sighed, once again looking into her beautiful eyes, and placed her head into the jar, the eyes seemingly focused on the label marked "Embalming Fluid". I thought to myself how great it would be having her back in her entirety. I also thought of the man who had done this to her. I thought of what he had done to ME.

I scooped up Brooklyn in my left arm, then went on my way towards the back yard, remembering the hidden bunker within the garden. I brushed the grass away, then lifted the heavy cover, the metal of it grinding against the concrete as it swayed back. I worked my way down to the main room of the bunker, then ran my fingers along the wall, looking for a light switch, then began waving my hand through the air, looking for a chord that would turn on an overhead light, finally finding one in the center of the room. Only one flickering bulb dimly lit the room, but I was comfortable. Quite to the contrary of my previous emotion to this room, I felt at ease. I looked around the room at the countless amounts of knives, left by the man who delivered my new scars, selected twelve from the wall, sat down at the desk with the sharpener, and began sharpening. I grinned at the thought of what would become of "Bob the Butcher", and sorted through the thoughts in my head as to what fate would be appropriate for a man such as he. Perhaps a mount of his head on my living room wall would be acceptable? I grinned. Soon his time would come. Soon I would take my next victim.

Bob the Butcher- Confinement

After I killed Brooklyn and marked my next victim, Daniel, I was captured. Not long after, but this was over a 40 year span of killings, torture, abduction, and crimes dark enough to make the pope vomit. Needless to say, the jury was swift with my punishment. I was taken to Smithland Penitentiary, with occasional visits to Smithland Mental Health Facility. The local doctors had an interest in my psychology, due to the hefty rap sheet that I had built up over the years, and wanted to set up monthly sessions for examinations. You may be curious what brought me to this chapter in my life, and you'd be right to wonder. I once had a family. A loving wife and a darling child. I was a highly respected doctor, one of the most sought after in all of New Jersey, and repeatedly requested for my assistance at the MAYO clinic in Minnesota. I was also a strong willed, yet empathetic person. That's why, when the situation would arise that a person could not be saved, co-workers would turn to me to deliver the message. Something I had heard fairly often throughout my career, was a fairly cold question that, no matter how many times asked, would penetrate me like a knife. "Why couldn't you save me? What will I tell my family?", they would say, and over time, I began to think to myself about how this must be the most painful part of their ailment, finding out that they could not be saved, and their families would be one member less.

I began to contemplate whether or not there would be a way to avoid this part of the process, and came to the conclusion, that in order to ease the pain, I would give them their release early. I gathered the chemicals I needed from the hospital after doing a bit of research on lethal injection. I collected sodium thiopental, pancuronium, and potassium chloride, then prepared myself to become an Angel of Death. I would work by slipping away from the house late at night while everyone was asleep, and silently walking the halls of the hospital late at night. I would claim that I was just doing a routine check up on the patients in intensive treatment, and once a night, three times out of the week, I would inject the chemicals into my patients. This way, it would look like they naturally died over night. Anymore, and someone might suspect my tampering. I continued with this process for ten years.

One day, a patient was sent in for an autopsy. You could imagine the coroner's state of alarm as he phoned the police. Once my chemicals were found in the veins, security was enhanced at the hospital. Unfortunately, I remained unaware until I fell victim. I went about my routine, stopping in at the hospital room of what would be my last patient. I collected the syringes, prepared the body, and before I could make the first injection, security stepped in, apprehending me and reporting me to the head of medical staff. I lost my license and was sentenced to twenty years in prison. I could not understand why I was taken away, or why I was being punished for saving another human from the pain they were enduring, but I dealt my time, and continued my work. You see, in prison, no one is happy. Everyone shuffles about with their day to day lives, waiting for the end of their sentence, or for an escape through death. That's where I came in. Once again, as night fell, I would trip the lock to my prison cell, and wander the halls of the great facility, seeking my next victim. I would trip the locks of cells, open the door, and carry in a few carefully smuggled in syringes filled with the chemicals that I had used during my work at the hospital. A few injections and my patients would receive the release they were seeking.

Eventually, the guards caught on to my tricks, and chose to punish me. Not by sending me to the hole, not by separating me from the others, but by trapping me in a cell with some of the bigger inmates in the facility, and letting them violently and savagely thrash me, breaking one arm, three ribs, my jaw, and one foot. This would become the last instant that I would let someone punish me for my work again. After all, I was working as a man of the people, bringing them release through death. I waited in the infirmary, waiting for my recovery, and once my recovery came, I tripped the lock on my cell for the last time, released a few suffering guards from their torment, and freed myself from the facility.

I darted down the gravel road leading away from the penitentiary for as hard and long as I could, and, about an hour later, I had finally reached town. I was exhausted. With almost no energy left to carry me anymore, I staggered toward the house that my family and I had lived in. I checked the doors to no avail, each was locked, and having enough respect for my family that I didn't want to disturb their slumber, I decided to sleep in the bunker located near the house in the back yard. I climbed down the ladder with the last of my energy that I could force, then fell asleep on the cold, concrete floor, impressively, still more comfortable than a prison mattress. I woke up the next morning to the sound of children, and what sounded like a birthday clown performing tricks for the crowd. I thought to myself and realized that today was my son, Alex's birthday party. I thought hard about what gift I would give him. I had no money for a new toy. I dug through boxes that were gathered around the large room, hoping to find something I could give him. Eventually, I came upon my gun, and a large hunting knife. The gun was a CZ 75. The light glimmered reflecting off of it's magnificent frame. I had found my new tools, and I had found the perfect birthday present for my son. I quickly climbed up the ladder, the gun tucked into a holster strapped to my left leg, the knife tucked into a sheath strapped to my right. I reached the cover of the bunker, turned it away from my exit, and stepped out.

The crowd looked at me with dissatisfied faces, the same way many looked at me. As if I was a monster. I had never expected this kind of reaction from my family. I thought that they would understand. Afraid, the children ran to my wife. I stared back at them, confused. Why was my son not happy to see me? Why not my wife? There was a time that they were the world to me, and I was the world to them. The expressions on their faces showed that it had been ripped away. Why? It was because once again, this was the punishment for doing the right thing, for providing assistance to those experiencing pain. Their reactions infuriated me, controlled me. Fueled by rage, I screamed at the top of my lungs and flipped the nearest table, holding the cake, presents, and gift bags toward the house. I shouted at them, trying to convince them that everything would be okay, they still didn't trust me. I paused, desperately trying to think of what I could do to comfort them, then approached the clown, deciding to show them just how I would help them find release. I grabbed him by the throat, then flung him to the ground, still in a fit of rage, but also in a state of panic, realizing how this must look. I pinned him to the ground, then drew a marker from my pocket. I began drawing dotted lines around the outside of his face, marking where I would begin the incision. I grabbed the knife from it's sheath, then began cutting. He screamed and struggled, but he would be free soon enough. He had passed out from the pain half way through, and began bleeding to death. I grinned, thinking of how good of an example I must have set. I peeled the face off of the clown, the tendons stretching along with the face, until finally they snapped and hung loosely from his facial muscles, then placed it over my own, in an attempt to look hospitable to the crowd. I rose slowly as not to scare them any more than I already had, then turned around to face them.

"See?" I replied with a grin across my face. "It will all be okay. Trust me."

I drew the gun from my holster, then smiled, thinking of how much I would be helping them. I pulled the trigger repeatedly, watching each party guest drop to the ground in release. I smiled once again, I had removed my family from their pains, their woes, and they deserved it, they were good people, after all. In the years after, I went on with my work, finding a person in need and releasing them from their trouble, but eventually I became corrupted. I started killing for different reasons. Not to help others, but to help myself. I developed a taste for the blood. I'd kill the healthy, strong, weak, young, old, whatever would satisfy my desire, but is that so bad? I've worked hard shedding people of their pained existence, wasn't it about time that I had my reward? Twenty years later, I killed Brooklyn and marked Daniel, only shortly after to finally be apprehended again. Now I sit here, in the Smithland Mental Health Facility, being examined by doctors and criminal psychologists as if I were a lab rat. My story is long, dark, and painful. I don't plan to tell any of it to the doctors. I plan to keep quiet, and let them know as little as possible. These are the people that hurt the innocent by preventing me from saving them, and now, are preventing me from finding satisfaction through the same method. I'm rotting away here, and soon I'll need to be free again.

"Hello, Mr. Elderson", a nurse said cheerfully, greeting me as she walked in. I remained silent and cold. I wasn't happy to be here and I wanted her to know that. "How are we today?", she continued with a smile.

"Confined", I replied, with as cold of an expression as possible. She sat with pen and clipboard in ready position, adamant on collecting the information she wanted. I sighed, then leaned back in my chair. "Alright, what would you like to know?" I asked.

"Well, I'd like to ask a generic question, and then expand on the topic.", she replied.

"Very well". She could tell by my replies that I wasn't enthused by any means.

"Alright, to get started, why did you do it?" She was right, the question was generic. One that I had heard millions of times. Judges, jury, doctors, they all seem to be eager about that one question.

"Simple," I replied, "I liked it.". She wasn't satisfied with my response. She wanted more.

"But why?" She persisted, "Did you find a need? Were you satisfying some lust or need to kill?"

"No, I just liked doing it.". She could tell she wouldn't get anywhere with this, and decided to ask another question.

"What can you tell me about your past, Robert?"

"It comes before the present, and it's not the future"

"I mean, what was growing up like?"

Realistically, growing up for me was just as uncomfortable as the present. I was trapped. I lived in a large house, never allowed to leave. I was home schooled, but not by my mother or father. Both were always away on business, leaving me in the company of maids and tutors, neither of which were well with children. However, I didn't have any siblings, so that left me with few options.

"I had just the standard, average family. My father was busy raising three boys. We were four men, living all together, and we were all alone. Then one day this fellow met a lady, and they knew this was much more than a hunch, that this group must somehow form a family, and that's the way we all became the...." The doctor scowled. Clearly she was not amused, she opened her mouth to interrupt, but without letting her, I butted in and continued, "THE BRADY BUNCH!"

She sighed, aggravated with my ruse, and stood up from her chair. "I think I need a break."

"Really?" I replied. "But you've only just arrived."

She exited the room without hesitation, leaving me sitting alone in the empty room with my thoughts. Several times now, that doctors have tried analyzing me, always to no avail, and it would stay that way. I watched the clock, shifting about in my chair, waiting for the doctor to return. About a half an hour had passed. Generally a doctor is only allotted five to fifteen minute breaks during an interview with a patient. Just as I stood up from the table, the lights in the interview room flickered, and with a bright flash, the room went dark. I walked towards the exit, expecting to be apprehended by the guards that are usually standing on the other side, waiting for just such an occasion, but to my surprise, they were gone. I stood alone in the empty hallway, which branched off into different parts of the building. No lighting here either, meaning the power must have gone out in the entire building, which, once again, didn't make much sense. A place like this generally has a backup generator for a situation such as this. The sound of escaped patients running wild echoed throughout the building.

From the sound of it, they had been freed from their cells. I would need a way to defend myself. I ventured through the hallways, trying to navigate my way to the kitchen, where I'd be able to find a few good sized knives. The sounds of screaming, frantic patients grew louder as I worked my way through the building, and as I moved forward, I began to notice gas flowing through the building. At first thought, it may have been smoke, but it had a bizarre stench that warned me otherwise. I covered my face with my shirt and did my best to avoid it, continuing my way through the building. I eventually found my way to the kitchen, and collected two of the biggest knives I could find. I moved forward to the next part of the building, the hallway leading to the main lobby, finding an army of freed patients running wild, attacking each other, harming themselves, pounding on the walls and calling at the doors like caged animals. I had worked with people long enough to know that even with the mentally ill, this was not normal behavior. The gas that was being pumped through the building was triggering some bad reaction. I suspected a trace of LSD might be somewhere in the mix. Nevertheless, I was only a few steps away from the exit, and this would be the day I would return to society.

I moved swiftly, but about half way down the hall, I caught the attention of one of the patients. His head rocketed up like a beast ready to attack. I knew if he reached me, he'd kill me. I braced myself as he charged towards me, screaming wildly, and, a few steps away, came to a halt, then collapsed to the ground, sliding across the checked floor towards me. I looked down at his now oozing body, and found three throwing knives jammed into the back of his head. I had seen these before. They belonged to me. I looked back up from the body, to see where the knives had come from. A dark silhouette stood in the middle of the hallways, looking back at me.

"He's mine." He said, in a deep, echoing, almost supernatural voice.

He continued approaching me, and I, him, in a state of confusion. He appeared to be wearing a tattered, torn black, hooded sweatshirt. He wore the hood up, the brim of the hood surrounding a gas mask that he wore over his face. Along his legs, he wore several sheaths which held several different knives of several different sizes, once again, all mine. My eyes returned to the mask, confused.

"What's the matter?" The voice rumbled, "You don't recognize me? Here, let me help."

He removed the mask slowly, revealing two empty eye sockets and an elongated face, attached to a broken jaw, hanging loosely and an unnaturally wide mouth. The mark I had left him with was apparent. It was Daniel.

"You thought I'd be your next victim, didn't you, Bob?" He continued, "I'll bet you didn't expect that I'd turn the tables on our game of cat and mouse."

This was premature game. He wasn't supposed to die yet. This wasn't how I had planned it. I grew angry. I was both furious over the thought that I had lost control over the situation, and that he was trying to stand me up. I was the reign master, he had no power over me, and it was foolish for him to think otherwise.

"You're weak", I replied, "You're too weak to take me. That's the way this works. I hold power over you, you become my victim, I take your life. You can't harm me."

He looked at me with an expression that challenged my last reply, then, with a flash, drew my machete from his leg holster. With the next second, he swung at me, almost striking me across the neck, but just skimming me as I ducked back.

"I'd like to put your theory to the test, Bob." He replied, coming at me once more. I charged back, knife prepared in my hand. He swung at me, but I ducked down, sliding across the floor on one knee, striking his leg while I slid, revealing more sheet white skin and a large gash protruding from it. I stood up and smiled at the thought that I could remove him from this earth that easily, and then looked back at his leg. Blood did not seep from the cut, instead a thin, black smoke rolled out. Astonished, I looked back at him, and with a whisper replied

"You're not human!"

He grinned wildly. "Now you're getting it."

He approached me, swinging consecutively with no hesitation, striking me multiple times across the arms and legs. Thick gashes rose up, and blood poured out like heavy rain. With my next act, I forced myself toward him, tackling him and forcing him to the ground. I drew a slit across his throat, hoping this would deter him. He smiled again, and with the machete still in hand, jabbed my leg deep. I screamed in pain, then fell back. I slowly rose from the ground, finding that I had lost use of my left leg. I thought quickly, in a state of panic. If I could find a lab, I might be able to give the same injections I had used to lay previous patients of mine to rest. If any part of him was still human, this would kill him. I began to run, limping with each step, but desperately fighting for my life. I was approaching the main office, when he caught up to me, placing one hand tightly on my shoulder, as quickly as I could, I spun around, jabbing my knife into his leg, crippling him and forcing him to the ground, he shouted out in pain as I continued running.

I entered the office and found the medical supply, then quickly began sorting through for what I needed. I was at a lack of supply, but found Sodium Thiopental, possibly the most helpful chemical I could find, if not all three. I loaded a surringe, and braced myself as he forced himself through the door, tackling me, the instant he struck me, I jabbed the needle into the gaping hole where is left eye once was, as he once again cried out in pain, then injected the fluid directly into his brain. He collapsed immediately, hitting the ground with a heavy thud. I was free to once again check through cabinets and drawers, looking for the rest of my supplies. Not long after, I had found vial's of both Pancuronium and Potassium Chloride, and made the final injections. His breathing grew heavy and rapid, before finally slipping away. I had finally taken my victim. He didn't manage to defeat me, but he was strong, much stronger than he was before. I had under estimated him. He was the man who, after all of my years of killing and victimizing, made me feel fear. Before leaving the asylum, I set fire to the building, making sure that I would never have to return to confinement.

Dan the Wanderer

Hazily, I woke up to the smell of smoke and the sight of flickering flames. My limbs burned intensely, my head was throbbing. The last thing I could remember was my fight with Bob, but could only remember segments. I sat up, then looked around the office. Vials and the syringe that I was injected with were scattered around me. Curious, I began reading the labels on the bottles. Sodium Thiopental, Pancuronium, potassium chloride. I was familiar with all of these. They're commonly used in lethal injection, which means I should be dead now. I couldn't understand how I was still alive, but I didn't have time to think. The building was burning down fast, and I needed to escape. I weakly picked myself up off of the ground, and limped, making my way through the main hall, and toward the front door. The sound of maniacs screaming in pain filled the air, and I passed by, watching as patients would flail about, burning alive, trying desperately to put out the flames. I made it out of the front door just before the building collapsed in on itself. I found the truck, creaked the door open, and drug myself inside. I sighed heavily, and rested my head back on the top of the seat. I thought I was prepared for him. I had the power of demons and he was still too strong for me. Nevertheless, I almost had him. With a little more practice, I would kill him.

I looked out through the windshield. The sun was setting just beyond the borderline of the trees. It was almost night time. I thought about what I would do next, and decided to go home, stitch my cuts and gashes, then return to town for some late night fun. I shifted the truck into drive, and the beast rolled towards the exit, then out onto the gravel road leading to town. An increasing pain rose from my stomach, reminding me that I hadn't eaten in days. I decided to stop by a small truck stop on the way home. Before stepping out of the truck, I slipped on my original mask, as to have a less startling appearance to the restaurant goers.

The cafe was old and dusty, as well as filled with old and dusty people, farmers, truckers, and rednecks, mainly. A wrinkled waitress greeted me with a raspy voice and showed me to my table. A window seat, giving me a nice view over the skyline of the town. She took my order and after, I sat watching out the window, lost in thought, observing the scenery. I took my eye sockets off of the window for a moment to glance around the restaurant. All eyes were on me. I decided to make no brash actions, as this would only attract more attention. Instead, I turned my sockets back to the window. The sun was setting just beyond the sky line, and children ran along the streets in an attempt to get home before the sun went down. Fewer cars rolled down the streets, and trucks rolled in through the entrance of the truck stop. Just then, I was ripped away by the voice of another customer in the truck stop, badgering me for my attention. It was a large man with a thick mustache and wrinkled, tan face. He wore a Farmall hat and a flannel shirt.

"Hey faggot", he said, in a harsh tone, "It ain't Halloween. What you wearin' that mask fer'?" I clinched my fist, trying desperately to ignore the simpleton.

"HEY!" he continued, even louder this time, "I'M TALKIN' TO YOU, BOY! WHY YOU WEARIN' THAT MASK?!"

I could tell that he wouldn't leave until I gave him the attention he wanted. I bit my tongue, trying not to cave his skull in, and finally spoke, "I don't want any trouble."

He only grew angrier, and more obnoxious. "You got trouble, boy! You think you can come into my place, wearin' that mask like you ain't got no damn sense about ya? YOU GOT TROUBLE!"

"What is it you want, sir?", I asked, losing my patience.

"I want you to either take that god damned mask off, or I'll take it off for you."

I wasn't going to be able to talk my way out of this, so it was time to handle this the way I wanted to since the beginning.

"I'm not taking my mask off. If you think you're man enough, you're going to have to make me. Be out back in five minutes. I'll be waiting to knock the rest of your teeth out."

He grinned, thinking he got his way, "It's about time you man up. Alright, I'll be out back. Hope you ain't much fond a' breathin'. You ain't gonna be doin' much of it when I'm done with ya."

He left the table, exiting the cafe and turning towards the back of the restaurant. Grabbing my glass, I stood up from my table, and walked to the back of the cafe, where the restrooms were, then began sorting through cupboards looking for cleaning agents. Generally, heavy duty cleaners contain sulfuric acid, which is quite a fond toy if you know how to use it right. I filled the cup with what I could find, then made my way out of the back door, where I found my favorite redneck, accompanied by two friends. They gathered around me, crowbars and tire irons in hands, and prepared to fight.

"We gonna beat some sense into you, faggot", one said, raising a crowbar to strike me.

With a flick of my wrist, a wave of acid splashed over their faces, sending each once into an intense pain, screaming for it to stop. I grabbed two blades from the sheaths on my pant legs, faced the backup fighters, and swung my arms, sending a thick gash across their throats. Lastly, targeting the trailer trash that originally approached me, I sent my boot to his chest with a heavy blow, knocking him down. I leaned in close to his face, then grabbed his hair with one hand.

"I'm going to teach you what happens when you fuck with the wrong people, you stupid piece of shit." I said, just before slamming his head back against the hard concrete.

Holding a knife in each hand, I jammed both directly through his eyes, piercing his brain. Blood errupted as his body went limp. I stood back up, then slid the knives back into their sheaths. I wasn't done just yet. These pigs had a lot of meat on their bones, and I didn't intend to let any of it go to waste. I drug each corpse to the back door of the restaurant, which was also near the kitchen. Carefully creeping in, I watched the cook vigorously working, preparing orders, much too busy to notice my entrance into the kitchen. I approached him from behind, and, without hesitation, slit his neck, and sent him to the floor in a puddle of blood, then began hauling each of the corpses into the kitchen. I cleared the counter to make way for one body, as I began reading the first order.

"One burger. Easy." I said to myself, as I drew a butcher knife from the counter, and began slicing flesh away from the body in layers.

Blood gushed out, and I smiled as I held out my fingers, caught a few drops with my fingertips, and began drinking. After trimming an appropriate amount, I approached the grinder and began inserting the meat. What was once rude, obnoxious, and crude, now became strings of crude, tainted, thick red meat. I padded the meat into a patty, then slid it onto the grill located in the center of the kitchen. As I cooked, a smell rose up that none of my senses have had the luxury of experiencing before. It was delicious, sweet, and my mouth watered as the smell of roasting meat filled the air. I continued cooking each order, making sure that each was backed up so that they would all arrive to their customers at the same time. After preparing each order, I left to the restroom, grabbed the bottle of cleaning agent once more, then splashed the solvent over the food I had prepared. I announced that the orders were ready, and once by one, customers began sinking their teeth into dumb, dumb, and dumber.

I smiled a wide smile, watching as, almost simultaneously, customer after customer dropped their food to their plate, and began choking. Foam rose up from their mouths, bubbling out as they clasped their hands around their throats, not understanding what had just happened. Then, the sounds of thuds rang throughout the restaurant as the heads of each victim crashed into the tables and plates, the bodies limp and lifeless. In a state of shock, each of the attendants working at the truck stop approached the kitchen, brimming with questions. I braced myself with my blades once more, as they burst through the kitchen door demanding an explanation. In one, smooth swipe, the blades sliced each neck, sending each of the attendants to the floor in a thick puddle of red. I slid my knives back into their holsters, then chuckled grabbing a burger off of one customer's plate while walking out. I took a big bite, grinning to myself. I had never tasted human before. It was delicious. Like pig, but more flavor. Stepping out of the door, I flipped the "open" sign to "closed", and climbed into my truck, ready to return home.

I rolled into the driveway around 10:00 p.m., exhausted. I flung the door open, dragging myself in, then plopping down my recliner in the living room. I reached into a basket sitting on the table next to the recliner, pulling out a needle and thread, then began sewing up the gashes from my escapade, the black smoke protruding from my leg began flowing in thinner and thinner puffs until finally, the cuts were sealed. I stared at the scar left from the cut, thinking to myself about the black smoke, flowing throughout my veins. I couldn't be killed, I couldn't bleed, I didn't think for myself anymore. Whatever I had become, it wasn't human. I stood up from my chair. I looked across the room, to the dining room table, Brooklyn's head still in place, eyes still fixated on the label marked "embalming fluid". I wondered how many lives I'd need to take before I could have Brooklyn back, in her entirety again. I stood up from my chair, scooped Brooklyn's head out of the jar, and returned to my bedroom, laying down comfortably, ready to sleep, cradling her head close to my chest.

In my slumber, I found myself in a dark place. Fire spread behind the silhouette of trees and mountains, and I stood in the middle of a dry plain, where nothing grew. The terrain was covered with dark soil in uneven mounds. In the distance I saw a dim light, which became increasingly bright with size. I squinted my eyes, focusing on the center of the light. In the middle sat a solid object, appearing to have human movements. Upon observation, I found this object to be human, charging directly for me. Panicking, I ran in the opposite direction, trying to escape, but to no avail. The unidentified person charged directly into me, sending me collapsing into to the ground, and then began slamming fists against my shoulders, neck, and head. I squirmed, rolling over to face my attacker. My eyes grew as I realized who this mysterious person was. Brooklyn sat above me, screaming in pain as fire seared her skin, throwing her now crisp and burnt fists against my chest. I stumbled back, trying to escape, only taking a few steps before observing the ground below her opening up. From the hole erupted thick flames, and the screams of a thousand tormented souls, while ropes launched out, wrapping themselves around Brooklyn like a marionette attached to strings. In that instant, she was pulled down, fast as lightning, screaming to escape. I ran after her, trying to save her, only to find that the hole had re-sealed itself before I could reach her.

I woke up, screaming at the sight of the horrible scene that I had witnessed. I looked down at Brooklyn's head. Still safe, cradled in my arms. I curled back up, trying to rest, but could only spend the rest of the night tossing and turning, unable to close my eyes for more than a blink. Days had passed and I'd find myself going through the same routine. Waking up, preparing myself for the day, slaughtering a few victims, nourishing myself with blood and flesh, then returning home, cradling Brooklyn while I fell attempted to sleep, but once again tossing and turning after horrific nightmares filled my slumber. In just the period of one week, my murder toll rose up to seventy people, but still with no reward. Brooklyn still remained incomplete, and I was growing impatient.

One night, after returning home from a day of gruesome slaughters, I flung my knives into the wall, furious. I plopped down onto my recliner, staring at Brooklyn's disembodied head with an angry scowl. Where was the reward for all of my work? Sure I enjoyed what I was doing, but I was being taken advantage of, and I couldn't have that. I was more than some tool. I thought long and hard about the intent of Ossairus and his followers. Why would they want all of these people dead? They seemed to be random people, of no convenience to he and his group. Why all the meaningless slaughters? My eyes darted around the room, searching for an answer, until it finally dawned on me. I focused on a crucifix that belonged to Brooklyn, left hanging as a decoration on the living room wall. I was working for a very diverse religious group, who clearly had no influence from God or a higher power. I couldn't be killed, and I was given my power through fire. I was working for the devil. Throughout the course of my work, I had been targeting the wrong people. I was chosen to destroy followers of faith.

I stood up from my chair quick, in a new state of enlightenment, then burst through the door and launched into the truck lightning fast. I threw the shifter into reverse, rolled back, then punched the accelerator, racing down the road way to the Smithland Church of Christianity. Tires squealed as I slid around turns, navigating my way through the town, finally arriving at the church. This would be it, I'd finally have Brooklyn back. I had to make my next act big, dramatic, I had to make sure that I would please Ossairus. I started by hauling a canister of gasoline from the passenger seat of the truck and making a circle around the church.

Acting quickly, I located the fuse box for the building, and pulled the master switch, shutting down power to the church. Through stain-glass windows, I could hear the quiet, confused whispers of church goers. Finally, stepping inside of the circle of gasoline, I pulled a zippo lighter out of my pocket, throwing it down, and watching flames erupt around the church. Screams filled the church as I stood outside of the front doors, removing my mask, waiting to greet the crowd. People trampled each other like cattle in a stampede, trying to find a direction to travel in. They found themselves trapped inside as the building caught fire, flames charged up the sides of the church, hungry for the victims inside. I watched the people spread as the priest of the church, Father Mccainey, stepped out, approaching me while holding a bible, quoting passages, and forcing a crucifix into my face. I grinned an evil grin, ripping the crucifix out of his hand.

"Might be a bad time to start preaching", I said, just before jamming the crucifix into his throat, sending him to the ground, clutching his neck.

Being too far from the nearest city, the nearest fire department was more than twenty minutes away, too far to arrive on time. The church became a volcano of fire, collapsing in on it's people, killing everyone inside. I walked through the flames, grinning wildly, padding out embers that tattered my shirt. I carried the priest over my shoulder, thinking of how pleased Ossairus would be to see the gift I had brought for him. I tossed the corpse into the passenger seat, then rolled down the road, traveling back to the house. The trip was long and painstaking, and I was impatient, thinking of how I'd finally hold Brooklyn in my arms again during the entire trip. As I approached the house, I found that the front door had been left wide open. The lock was torn out of the frame. Someone had broken in. I left the priest in the truck, running into the house making sure that nothing was stolen. Everything appeared to be intact, but when I turned to face the kitchen table, my heart sank, for I then realized that Brooklyn's head was missing. Panicking, I went with the first thought that popped into my mind. She was taken by Ossairus.

I ran back out into the driveway, pulling the corpse out of the passenger seat quickly, flinging it over my shoulder and charging into the forest in the direction I felt I was drug in when I happened upon Ossairus and his followers. I walked deeper and deeper into the forest, for what seemed like hours, until I finally reached a clearing where I felt was my destination. My heart stopped as I looked at what I had believed to have been the gathering place for Ossairus and his followers, but instead, finding a large crack running through the center of the forest. Flames erupted out, tickling the sky, and between the flames ran several long ropes. My eyes traveled up the ropes to the top, to where my astonishment, I found Ossairus, his followers, and Brooklyn, all attached to the ropes like marionettes. Brooklyn was complete once again, her heard sewn back to her torso crudely. Shocked, I dropped the priest, and watched as her jaw dropped up and down in an irregular fashion as she spoke, sliding up and down like a gate.

"DANIEL!", she cried out, "HELP ME! IT HURTS! OH GOD, HELP MEEEE!"

I stumbled forward, my jaw agape, not believing what I was experiencing. At my feet, six more ropes shot up, connecting to each of the priests limbs, then in a flash dragging him into the crack and through a mountain of flames. I didn't care. I had to rescue Brooklyn. As carefully as possible, I gripped one rope, swinging to the next, then to the next, working my way towards Brooklyn. Finally, I had reached her rope, and began working my way up. I grabbed her legs, then pulled my way up to her torso, and began cutting the ropes around her arms one by one with a bowie knife. I paused, looking into her dull, glass eyes. All traces of realism had left them. She almost seemed false, like a mannequin. Her jaw began swinging again. My heart raced as I watched her speak.

"Daniel....babe....is that you?" she asked, in a timid voice.

"Y-yes?" I replied, looking into her eyes. Her brow sank, scowling at me, yet grinning the same wild grin that I wore many times building up to this day.

"GO TO HELL" she said bluntly, plunging her finger tips into my chest, striking in a circle around my heart, and then ripping it out violently. I felt my vision fading, but not before looking down at my chest and noticing ropes approaching my legs, connecting to each of my limbs, then dragging me down at a frightening speed. I felt flames engulf my body with an intense heat, as I screamed in pain. I looked up, watching the crack at the surface of the hole drift away with my life.

"Welcome to Hell!", my mind echoed.

Lucifer's Puppets

Daniel's body ripped through layers of hell at a frightening speed, seeming to grow faster as he shot down. The screams of a thousand torments echoed around him as he traveled, only to finally come to a stop when his body crashed onto an operating table with a loud "THUD!". The marionette strings that brought him here wrapped around the operating table and his torso, removing his ability to move. Daniel's eyes darted around the room in terror. He knew where he was, and he didn't like it. He knew that he had the notion that he was getting himself into trouble when he struck his deal with Ossiarus.

The room Daniel landed in seemed to go on forever in all directions. The center of the room was dimly lit, revealing only a checkered floor, and the operating table Daniel rested on. Out of the corner of Daniel's eye, he watched as a black smog like figure took form beside the table, shifting into the shape of a man with long dark hair, a black business suit, yellow eyes, clean white teeth, and a goatee. The man towered over Daniel tremendously, hunching over like an adult speaking to a child.

"Well if it isn't Mr. Daniel Berger. At long last we meet." The man said, in a dark, bellowing tone.

"What the hell is this?!" Daniel questioned, forcing about, trying to free himself from his binds.

"Oh Daniel, you know what this is, you foolish child. You're in Hell. You've become a pawn in my game, and now that I've used you to my liking, it's time to get rid of you."

"FUCK YOU!" shouted Daniel, before spitting in the face of the devil.

Lucifer did not take this lightly. With a forceful strike, he slammed Daniel's head against the table with a crack that seemed to echo throughout the room. "AHHH!", Daniel screamed out in pain, wincing, wishing that his hands were free so that he could hold his head. "Lucif....You're Luci.."

"Of course. Lucifer. Who did you think Ossiarus was speaking of when he told you he worked in association with the 'dark lord'?" Lucifer's smile grew, stretching across his face like a lightning bolt across the sky.

"Who is Ossiarus?" Daniel asked, dazed and filled with questions.

"Very well, you're confused. I shall inform you of everything that has happened building up to this moment, being that you're too simple minded to wrap your head around it. Ossiarus is the leader of a religious group centered around me. The group was founded in the early 1600s, I believe. They call themselves "Lucifer's Puppets". A bit cliché', but I like the name. Lucifer's Puppets would pledge their every whim to me in a sacred ritual, which would take place in thick forests at the beginning of the cycle of the moon. Each of the members would tie themselves with rope, attaching each end to their limbs like marionette strings. At the end of each rope, a pentagram would be drawn. The participants would wait inside of the pentagram while their bodies would fade away until death came. Once that time came, I had complete control over them. There's still a piece of them alive inside of each of their bodies, and that's how I was able to gain control of you. They're excellent at deceiving victims into falling into my ploy. The night you found yourself in the woods, broken and desperate for help, we found you and saw you're ailment as an advantage. The ritual that you took part in shredded your human existence, and gave you a new one, one of the demons. With that power, only one being on this planet could lead you to death, which is me. Now that you've completed your objective, I no longer find a use for you. I hope you don't think for a minute that I plan on making your demise easy for you,. simply because we're business partners." With that, gray skinned, sunken eyed, winged demons appeared at each corner of the operating table, wheeling it towards the darkness of the room. "WAIT!" shouted Lucifer. Daniel cocked his head back, to stare at him. "I almost forgot, your little treasure. Brooklyn."

Daniel looked up from where he had fallen. Like spiders legs, marionette strings lowered Brooklyn down. Her long black hair, flowed out as she moved, and her eyes glowed yellow, like Satan's. She wore a black leather dress, showing her curves, and her skin was a pale white. Once reaching the ground, she wrapped her arms around Lucifer, and Lucifer threw his arm around her. Daniel vomited as he watched the love of his life plant her lips against Lucifer's cracked, lizard like lips, then massage her tongue against his long-forked tongue. She looked at him with an evil stare and a bitter smile, as did Lucifer.

"Sorry Dan, guess the necrophilia was a bit of a turn off for her. She's mine now!"

Daniel screamed curses, attempting to kick his way free from the bed, but to no avail. Daniel, on the operating table, and the demons that wheeled him away faded into the darkness, as the screams of Hell's torment grew louder.

Ben

I marched through hell, the sounds of screams of many a victim echoing like music to my ear. My eyes centered on the large castle that stood in the center of it all. Dark and powerful, Satan's tower stood, guarding all of Hell. I arrived at the front door to be greeted by two, large, muscle baring demons wearing metallic helmets that hid their faces. They stepped aside, and I opened the main doors and followed the hallways to the main chamber where Satan and his queen's thrones were placed, where I found Satan and Brooklyn, now Na'amathe, waiting for me.

"Ben! My son!" Lucifer bellowed out, greeting me with a strong hand shake and a fatherly pat on the back.

"Good to see you're finally out of the asylum."

"Yes father, all thanks to you. For a place of healing, I think I left more insane than when I went in!"

"That wasn't my doing, my son", replied Satan, looking down into my face. "That's our wild card, the one that I don't have control over. Robert Crouse, a very powerful man, for someone who's a mere human. Even my star player, Daniel, with the power of the demon was defeated by him."

"Do you wish to dispose of him, father?"

"Not yet, my son.", said Lucifer, in a businessman tone. "Do you have the other lunatics under your control?"

"Yes", I replied, with an air of excitement flowing across my face. "They were easy to manipulate. They always are. Show them you have power, and they're all yours."

"Excellent!" replied Lucifer, his voice echoing throughout the chamber, "Use them to your advantage. Bring this "Bob the Butcher" to me. He may be a valuable aspect in our expansion."

"Immediately!", I replied, as bat-like wings began to protrude from my back. With one solid launch, I sliced through the window overlooking the realm of hell and launched myself to the surface, back into Smithland. I soared through the skies, scoping out my minions, finding them waiting just on the edge of the forest, then lowered myself to the ground to greet them.

There were four of them. David, aka "Bunny man Dave" is a mute who stands at six foot five. He was brought into the asylum after slaughtering twenty children one Halloween night. When apprehended, he was found clutching a bunny in his arm, while also wearing a rabbit mask, the same one he wore today. Then there's Mallard.

Mallard stands about my height. Since freed, he has skinned off all of his flesh and is missing one arm, leaving him a naked mass of walking tissue and muscle. Mallard suffers from extreme cases of schizophrenia and etomophobia, a dangerous combination to himself. When Mallard was first brought in, he was in an extreme need of skin graphs. Before apprehended, he skinned one of his arms and half of his torso, claiming that insects crawled beneath his flesh and needed to be removed. Next is Fantasia. Fantasia is a libidinous woman, with long black hair, black eyes, and silky smooth skin. She was brought in for both cannibalism and nymphomania. When questioned why she would have activity and eat her victims, she'd only reply "I like to play with my food." Last is Jeremiah. Jeremiah was brought in after he was accused of stealing corpses form a cemetery. Jeremiah has taken part in many Voodoo and Satanic rituals, giving him the skill of raising the dead with the correct ritual. Jeremiah was a slender person, standing just taller than Mallard, with long black hair, green eyes, and a bony face.

All were found to have qualities that could provide assistance in the expansion of Lucifer's empire, so all were recruited for the project. All are completely unaware, and until plans change, they shall remain this way. They all gathered around me upon my arrival, awaiting orders. As customary for her, Fantasia threw her arms around me and hung around my neck as I began my instructions.

"Is anyone familiar with the fellow who set fire to the asylum?"

"Yes", Mallard spoke up, always the intellectual of the group, "As soon as I had the chance, I began collecting as much information on the character as possible. His name is Robert Crouse, once a highly sought after doctor, now a murderous psychopath."

That's what I liked about Mallard, he was always the informant. Always curious about the world around him, he'd collect any information necessary to learn.

"You want us to kill him?", Fantasia said, breathing on my neck.

"No", I replied. "I want you to bring him to me. He could prove as a valuable asset to us."

All nodded in agreement. I dispatched the group and sent them on their way. Later that night, we would meet once again to discuss our progress. Of course, each of them were psychopaths, so we would not obtain our goal immediately, but in due time.

<u>Mallard</u>

He thinks I don't know. That son of a bitch.
Once freed from the asylum, the others
came to me for a leader to guide them. I
happily accepted, but to Ben's disapproval.
To set an example for who was "really in
charge", he ripped my arm off in front of the
group. I remember the cracking and
snapping sound my arm made as it
dislocated from my shoulder and the sound
of tearing flesh as I began to bleed out. He
takes me for a fool, but I know what he is,
I've done my homework. It'll only be a
matter of time until I'm leader again, and
once I'm back, I'll cut his eyes out and keep
them as my trophy. He'll pay for what he did
to me. Just like the others who have dared
to cross me.

When I was first brought into this
asylum, I was brought in for self-inflicted
wounds and schizophrenia, which had

developed from severe abuse at an early age. During my younger years, I was a very unpopular child. My parents hated me, and the other children hated me. The day usually began with me being drug off to school after a few strikes across the face from my mother, who, at the time was a ragging alcoholic, and was never satisfied with having to drag herself out of bed to bring me to school. Once she dropped me off, the next level of torment began.

As I said, I very disliked by my classmates. So, every day after lunch, during recess or whenever they found the time, they would drag me out away from the playground, away from the visibility of the teachers, so that they could pummel me. After said abuse, they'd gather in a pack of four. Three of them would hold my limbs down and head back, preventing me from being able to move, while another would pick as many insects as he could find to force down my throat. I had an extreme aversion to insects, which, unfortunately, was unable to stay hidden. This would happen to me on a regular basis, usually at least twice, or three times a day, and I'd be forced to ingest things like praying mantis, spiders, crickets, slugs, roaches, beetles, and anything else that they could find. The day would end with me returning home, both my father and my mother being awake this time, but still hung over, ready to beat the living shit out of me. Once they were finished, I'd spend the rest of the night throwing up every insect I was forced to eat that day, and studying my school books.

Eventually, I had graduated and was finally free to move away from all of the nasty people who would torment me. Everything was off to a good start after. I went to college, met a beautiful girl there named Abigail, fell in love, and set foot on the path towards the life that I had always wanted, although, I could never shake the feeling that the insects were still there. I never knew how or where, until one night when Abigail had fallen asleep in my arms. I sat there, cradling her and staring at the dark ceiling, until I felt a tickle on my arm. It began working it's way up from my hand and up my arm. I reached for it, and found that it was a roach. I panicked, and swatted it away. Where had it come from? Unless...They're INSIDE of her! YES! OF COURSE! I knew that I could help her.

We shared the same aversion to insects, and I didn't want her to suffer the same way that I had so many years ago, so I began by restraining her. I then retrieved some sleeping pills from the kitchen and slid each of them delicately into her throat, assuring that she wouldn't wake up during the process. I retrieved a knife and made my beginning insertion on her face. I began carving away at the skin, revealing tendons and muscle, and as I did, I could see dozens of insects pouring out of all kinds. I continued my work, and then pulled back the layer of flesh from her face. Next, I worked my way down to her torso. I carefully pulled off the night dress from my sleeping angel, revealing her naked torso. Such fine, milky skin, yet such a dark, disgusting thing underneath. I continued my work, and had finished a few hours later. I sat back and gazed at her skinless body. She no longer had her beautiful silky flesh, but I had finally set her free.

Then I looked at my arms. MORE INSECTS! They came scattering from every direction, some even slipping out from underneath my fingernails, which could only mean one thing. They were inside of ME as well! Living inside of me all these years and waiting to come back just when I felt I was free! I plunged the knife into my skin and began carving away at my flesh, not caring about the pain, each layer sliding to the ground like sheets of paper. I was half way through, and flesh remained on a straight line scaling the midsection my skin when she awoke.

She looked at me with panicked eyes at the sight of what I had done, then touched her face. She took a moment to feel her open tendons and muscle, then looked at her arms and back at me. She cursed my name, then ran out of the room and phoned the police. I was arrested and taken to the Smithland Mental Health Facility, where I began treatment, but to no avail. I still saw the insects. They were still there, and eventually, I'd finally have cut the rest of my flesh away and freed myself form their disgusting presence.

<u>Jeremiah</u>

I can feel it. It'll only be a matter of time until I can chant those sacred words again. Oh, how I long to hear them leave my lips once more. The dead have a place on this earth, you know. It's far more than just the dirt that covers it. Smithland is the perfect place for my deceased brethren and I. I can see it now, armies of the undead marching up and down each street, invading every home, scattering the woods by hundreds, and we'll keep growing in numbers. Smithland, where the dead don't stay buried.

This is what I was raised into, and every piece of it was true.

I was born into a family of gypsies. My mother was a voodoo priestess, and as such, I was given all of the customary rituals during my birth. I was home schooled, and during my upbringing, was taught everything voodoo, especially how to raise the dead. My mother was a sweet woman, and I loved her dearly. Eventually, she grew old and passed away, and in her passing, passed the title of voodoo priest unto me. I found myself deeply troubled by her death, and as a means of coping, I joined the army. I spent seven years working in the military, and eventually returned to Smithland. Upon my return, I found myself, once again, wrapped with depression over my mother's death, and eventually, came to the conclusion that I had tried oh, so hard to avoid.

I collected everything I would need, my book of rituals, a homemade rattle wrapped in leather, and the poison of a puffer fish, returned to my mother's grave, and performed the ritual necessary to bring her back. She returned as something lesser. She was there, yes, but only physically. She didn't speak, her eyes were rotted out, her skin sagged, and still had the appearance of cloth stretched over wire, but I loved her. She became an inhabitant at my house, and I would care for her, feed her, and bathe her, but one night, when I went to the store to retrieve supplies, she broke out through the front door.

When I found her, she was shot dead by the police. They explained that she attacked an elderly woman who was out walking her dog. The remains of both my mother and the woman were hidden under two plastic tarps preventing them from being exposed to the public. I was wrapped with grief. Now, without my mother, I was all alone, but I did it, I brought a person back from the dead. I could do it again. I could find a new family. I continued my practices, bringing a new member into the house each day, until the police found out about my activities. They called me insane. They didn't understand. So they sent me to Smithland Mental Health Facility, where I'd begin awaiting my return to society again, where I could finally return to my family, the living dead.

Fantasia

It's been years since I've eaten, since I've tasted the sweet flesh of another human being. I can recall the first time I ate. I was in college, on my way to becoming a lawyer. I had been moderately less lustrous back then, and I had settled down with a fiancé. One night, during sex, he came up with a new idea. He wanted to try experimenting with knives in bed.

He had always been one to lust after pain, and wanting to satisfy, I didn't refuse. I grasped the long blade that he handed me, and with his instruction, began cutting through layers of skin. He groaned with excitement, as did I. I watched blood ooze from his body in small waves. I found it incredible. I continued cutting, and refused to yield when he asked me to stop. I'd cut deeper and deeper each time, the waves of blood growing thicker and thicker with every cut. Finally, his body was covered in thick gashes, and he passed away. His eyes sat vacant in their sockets, staring at the ceiling. I realized what I had done. I had killed the one I loved. The one I was engaged to, the one I was supposed to marry. I couldn't take the pain of separation. I couldn't stand the thought of knowing that we'd be separated once I was taken away for murder and his body was buried, so I did the first thing that came to mind. I drug his body to the kitchen, and prepared it to be eaten. I prepared him like one would a pig, separating the ribs and different slices of meat, then frying them over the stove and cooking them in the oven. Once the cooking was complete, I devoured his remains and smiled to myself. Now we wouldn't have to be separated. Now we could stay together. Time has passed now, and I've fallen victim to my desires. Killing, eating, fucking. Now that I'm free, it's finally time to feast again.

Bunnyman Dave

I still recall the day that they first started calling me "insane". I was a grade school teacher. Loved by many of the parents and children, and I had grown quite fond of each of them. One of the pros of being a teacher, is eventually, you get to start teaching your own children in school. I had two children; both were twins, one girl, Jessie, and one boy, Rodney. When I had them as students, they were twelve years old. I recall how we'd make jokes each day during class and how I'd single them out to be picked on, showing a special family love that made the room light up each day. I had a lovely wife, Sandra, who had been working as a nurse. I loved my family, and I loved my life.

However, one night, Sandra and I had gotten into an argument. I can't recall exactly what it was, but it was bad enough that she left the house, taking Jessie and

Rodney with her. Little did any of us know, this would be the last night I'd see any of them. You see, it was late winter, and the roads were slick. I assume, in her frustration, she didn't see the patch of ice that drove her car into a head on collision with a semi. The crash was horrible. Sandra died on impact, but Rodney and Jessica were still alive, oozing blood by the bucket full. Before help could arrive, both had bled to death.

The next few days were horrible for me. Each day I'd wake up alone, eat breakfast alone, and go to work, missing having the ability to tease my children. My students were sympathetic, and I believe I received an apology from each of them. They and their parents showed up to the funeral. In the time that had passed, I grew to hate the sight of my students. They became a cruel reminder of what many of the parents of Smithland had, and what I could never have again.

Eventually, I decided to put an end to what they had. I came into class with a rabbit mask on. A cheap, plastic rabbit mask that I had used one Easter to entertain our children. I explained to each of them that I had met a rabbit breeder a few miles out of Smithland, and we'd be visiting him and his rabbits today. Their faces lit up with excitement, as did mine, but both for entirely different reasons. I watched as the class assembled, then walked out towards the buses in an orderly line, whispering to each other about the upcoming field trip. Luckily, before we had arrived, I managed to locate the key for one of the busses and loaded my tools onto it. I latched the emergency door firmly from the outside to prevent any possibilities of escape. The children took their seats, and I slid into the driver's seat casually, shifting into drive, then rolling out of the school parking lot, taking the road that lead past the school, and then driving down a gravel road.

I followed the road with plenty of time, making sure that I found a location where little traffic had passed and few houses remained. Once I made my choice, the bus rolled to a stop, and I shifted into park. Confused whispers filled the bus, as the kids looked at each other, trying to make sense of why we stopped here. I grinned a sickening grin, then turned to the class.

"Do you miss Rodney and Jessie too?" I asked. No replies, but a look of dread rose from their faces along with the presence of confusion.

"Maybe it's about time that you finally joined them." I said, dragging a chainsaw out from underneath the driver's seat, pulling the chord and sending the motor roaring to life. The sounds of screams and the revving sound of the chainsaw's motor filled the air. Kids in the back began trying to force the door open, but to no avail. I worked my way from the front of the bus, to the back of the bus, severing limbs, heads, and splitting torsos in half, blood washing over me as I cut down each of them with a delightful burning, fueling sensation in my heart. I reached the end of the bus, and turned to see my masterpiece. Blood and disembodied limbs filled the cab and blood covered the walls. I then dropped the chainsaw to the ground, the motor dying as it landed. I took a seat on the bus, and tilted my head back, resting my eyes for only a moment.

When I opened them again, I saw the flashing lights of police cars rolling down the gravel road towards the bus. I did not resist. I had committed a crime, and found satisfaction through it. I was arrested and charged with insanity, easy break for the homicide of twenty-six children. I was sent to Smithland Mental Health Facility, where I would await the day that I'd be set free again, and finally be able to, once again, take the lives of more children and reveal the pain that I had experienced to more and more families.

Bob the Butcher-Post Arson

It has been three months since Smithland Mental Health Institute was burned to the ground. The town is run amuck with lunatics and murderers. No one is safe here, but no one can leave. After burning down the asylum, I took refuge around the town, a different place each night. This was before the murders began. There was no contact with the communities near Smithland, and we had no fire department or police station of our own, so once blood began to flow through the streets and splatter the walls of Smithland, I knew I had to find real shelter. I retreated to the house I had lived in so long ago to take refuge, only to find that it had burned to the ground.

However, nothing remained, except rubble, and in the center of it all, a small wooden marionette puppet made to look like a court gesture. It wore a three pointed hat of yellow, red, and purple with bells that dangled at the ends of each point, a costume that matched the pattern of the hat, a green mask with black eyes behind it, and a wicked grin that stretched to the carved cheek bones of the head unnaturally. I decided to keep it, as a memento of my newest victim, Daniel, and continued to the back yard, to my bunker. Luckily, this was still intact. I've lived there for two months now, keeping myself entertained through sharpening my knives and carrying on imaginary conversations with my new puppet. Occasionally, a time would come that I'd need to restock my food supplies. I'd arm myself with a bowie knife, a hunting knife, a hatchet, and a handgun before taking to the street. I'd listen to the rustle of grass as I'd make my first steps onto the lawn outside of my bunker, and began walking slowly and quietly to the streets.

Smoke filled the streets like smog. Houses would be locked at night, and those foolish enough to enter the streets without good reasons would often find themselves killed. Hell, I couldn't say that those that stayed in their houses were safe either. You see, even though every house would be locked up tight every night and still secured during the day, the children of Smithland all seemed to disappear. Parents began searching for their children, and while wondering the streets, would often meet their fate through a grisly murder. Disembodied heads, mutilated torsos, and thick puddles of blood would fill the streets of the once peaceful community. I take lives myself, yes, but there are some things that were never meant to happen. An entire community under siege and me fighting for my life, for example. It had been two weeks since I picked up supplies, and I was running low on water and food. I grabbed the usual, hunting knife, hatchet, bowie knife, and handgun, and set out on my way.

I listened carefully to my surroundings as I stepped out of the bunker, the only sound to be heard was the rustle of the grass under my boots as I slowly made my way to the streets. No one in sight, but a scream carried from across town. I'd have to be careful and be prepared. I had made it three blocks when, out of the smoke rolling across the street, I saw the silhouette of a thin, spiny man making his way towards me. Once spotting me, he stopped, staring at me for about a minute, while I stared back. He broke eye contact as he made a dead charge towards me. I'd have to make sure that I wouldn't make too much noise, as to not attract more attention. As he neared me, I quickly ripped my hatchet out of it's holster, and flung it at him, striking him directly in the forehead and sending him to the ground with a thump as his body bounced off of the concrete. I made my way towards him, then stepped on his neck, grabbed ahold of the hatched, and pulled back, his skull making the usual bloody, slick sound as I drew it out and back into my sheath.

I continued on my way, and eventually made it to the store. In a rush, I began stocking supplies, canned foods, water, and meat, and made my way out. Upon entering the street, I had a stroke of luck. There, across the street from the grocery store, sat a gray, discarded, 84' Chevy truck. The door was left open, and blood dripped from the driver's seat, giving the notion that the driver had been attacked. I made my way to the truck and checked the ignition for the keys. Success. I loaded my supplies into the passenger seat, slammed the door shut, and began cranking the ignition. It took a bit for the car to turn over, but at least now I had transportation. I shifted into drive, but before turning in the direction to head home, I thought to myself about my previous attempts to leave this town.

In the past, I have asked myself the same question I'm sure many have asked already, why haven't I left yet? The last time I tried leaving Smithland, I was on foot. I set foot just outside of the town late one night, and walked for two hours without looking back. I was overfilled with joy at the thought of being able to move on to the next town, maybe find an unused house, and begin as healthy of a life as possible. But, to my dismay, even through two hours of walking, when I finally turned back, I found that I had made no more progress than half a mile. Now that I had a truck, I could travel faster, further, and spend more time on the road. I decided to set a new experiment, heading in the opposite direction on the main road that led through town. I shifted into drive, and began to roll past the many destroyed, burned, and warped buildings, making my way through town, and finally hitting the gravel road that led out of town. Coincidentally, this was the same road that I had walked after burning down the asylum, one of my biggest mistakes, but the chilling reminder of what I had brought onto myself no longer stood, so I could travel without having anything to make me look back....Or so I thought.

I drove a few miles out of town until I saw something that made my heart stop. The Smithland Mental Health Facility, standing in the exact area and looking exactly the same as it was before it burned to the ground. It made little sense to me. No construction equipment had been in and out of town since the fire, and few dared to set foot out on the streets with enough time to repair it. The parking lot sat empty, and, letting my curiosity get the better of me, I took a spot at the front of the lot. The building stood tall and ominous, towering over me, standing in a position that almost seemed to say "I have power over you". The front door slid open with ease, and the entire building looked almost new, as if nothing had changed since the building burned down, except for the large vacancy that filled the building. I decided that this was a great time to explore. If the town had decided to reconstruct and bring each of the patients back in, it would be useful to map out every possible exit so that I could escape once more.

The hallways echoed with each of my footsteps, the sound carrying heavily throughout the building. I entered the building through the main hall, and decided to begin mapping the second floor first and work my way down. I made my way through the building, finding everything seemingly untouched. Each desk was in place, each cell had a mattress, chair, and glass encased television. I stepped inside one of them, which was replicate of a cell that I had stayed in once, the night before interviews with the doctors here. I found the television on, switched to a blank channel, static fluttering throughout the screen, the sound drizzling out like an electronic, indecipherable language. I switched off the TV, allowing a vacant sound of nothingness to enter the room and revealing a distant crash on the other side of the building. I grasped my bowie knife in my fist and slowly continued on, being careful not to make more noise than I did entering the building. I scaled the second and first floors, not finding anyone else there, only the occasional glimpse of shadows out of the corner of my eye, which I had brushed off as being animals that had gotten in during reconstruction. Lastly, I needed to inspect the basement.

I slowly made my way down, making sure to make light footsteps as to not carry on more sound throughout the building, and eventually found myself in complete darkness. I reached into my pocket and drew out an old, chrome flashlight that I had kept in my bunker for just such an occassion. I switched on the light, and only found myself rewarded with a few feet of visibility. I felt my path with my fingertips, and drug my feet in an attempt to prevent myself from tripping over anything. I eventually found myself in a long hallway, filled with hazmat suits and a dimly flickering light. At the very end of the hallway stood a heavy, rusted, metallic door left partially open. I reached the door, forcing it open and making my way into the next room, finding myself in an even thicker amount of darkness than before. The flashlight proved useless.

The first step in was a high drop into a pool of warm unidentifiable liquid. I began making my way through the room, dragging my hands along the walls trying to find a light switch. As my hand drug along the wall, I felt them cake in more thick, warm, liquid. Inaudible whispers began to fill the room, and the chemical encased my forearm as I ventured on, finally reaching a light switch. As the light switched on, I stumbled back in shock. The floor was pooled with deep blood, and every corner of the room was painted blood red. At all corners of the room stood the missing children of Smithland, all with a variety of missing limbs, eyes, broken jaws, slashed torsos, and all began moving slowly in my direction. I stumbled into the center of the room, watching the injured offspring surround me. My eyes darted up, noticing movement on the back wall of the room.

The figure of a man stepped out of it's camouflage. It revealed itself to be completely made up of muscle, blood and bone with no outer skin. It was missing an arm, and gritted it's teeth as it moved, sloshing through the thick pool of blood towards me. It extended it's one arm towards me, trying to reach out to me. Acting quickly, I grabbed his arm, swung back behind him, kicked both of his legs out with a swing of my own, and forced him to the ground. He began bobbing and weaving about, trying to escape as he began to drown. I held him down until his body finally became lifeless and ragged, then stood up to find myself once again surrounded by the children. Each of them began climbing up my arms and torso, dragging me down to the ground and forcing me to collapse backward into the blood. "Help me!" they all chimed, buzzing like angry bees throughout the room. They moved slowly, but with strength like zombies, then began drawing each of my blades from their holsters. I kept forcing my torso up to collect air and cough out blood that I had swallowed, only being forced down again. The last time I rose out, I was stabbed in the shoulder with my bowie knife, which dug deep, striking into the bone. I screamed out in pain, then was forced back down, once again choking and gasping for air. I felt more knives penetrate my body, striking me in the chest, legs, and arms. I began fading fast, and, with little strength left, I forced myself through the crowd, shoving through the children and flinging myself out of the room. I slammed the door behind me, and reached for a barely visible lock, encased in the darkness of the room. I could hear the banging of little hands against the metallic door, and I limped away without looking back, only thinking of what might happen if they got free.

I had to continue on through. I was losing blood and needed to find the medical ward of the sanitarium and stitch my wounds. I stumbled down the hallway, making my way past the many hazmat suits, and once again, into darkness. I had dropped the flashlight into the pool of blood and had no way of finding my path. I held my hands out in front of me, bracing myself to find the railing leading to the stairwell that would bring me back to the surface, but continued wondering, finding myself more and more lost. Eventually, I had led myself into another room in the basement.

A large, dark room, completely encased in darkness, other than a small flame that bobbed and weaved about as it made it's way towards me. The flame came to a halt in front of my face, and an embrace came from behind me. Bare women's breasts pressed against my back, and fingers began rimming around the outsides of my wounds, eventually forcing themselves into the gashes, drawing out blood, and bringing up blood to velvet lips that sucked them in smoothly. In a sentuating tone, a voice that seemed to carry from all corners of the room echoed out "Mmmm. Hey Dinner.", followed by a disturbing cackle that only the insane can imitate. I spun around to find a nude woman, with long black hair and dark eyes, licking my blood from her fingers, then wandering back towards me. She outstretched her arms, revealing a knife in one hand. Without hesitating, I dodged the swipe of the knife and landed a punch to her face. She collapsed to the ground, then looked back up at me, speaking through her teeth as she grumbled "Shit head", wiping a bloody lip with her arm. I kicked up the knife that she had, then grabbed her hair, forcing her up. I was only able to press the silver sleeve of metal against her throat before being struck against the wall from an unknown force that had came from behind her and rammed against my face.

It was powerful, stronger than a human, and through the faint light that the match had produced, I could see an unnatural form spreading throughout the room. I dodged what appeared to be oversized spiders legs, working my way throughout the basement, until finally; I tripped on the first step that led out of the basement. I charged up the stairs with great speed, my feet carrying sounds like machine guns as I ran. I reached the first floor and made it half way down the hallway when I found a plus shaped sign marking where the medical ward was located. I forced the door open, located a first aid kit, and began making my way out of the asylum when I was confronted by the creature that challenged me in the basement.

It was a thin man with long, black, flowing hair. He had a pale complexion and yellow eyes. He wore a business suit, and was suspended high into the air by the spider legs protruding from his back, the same legs that had forced me against the wall during my attack in the basement. He sped toward me, and, not knowing how to act, I raced towards him. He prepared one of the front legs to strike, as I fell back, sliding underneath him and grabbing a hold of the other front leg. As my weight drug along the floor, I tugged, forcing him to collapse face forward into the ground. Coming to a halt, I jumped back up to my legs, climbed onto his back, and sent a slash across his face with the silver knife I had collected in the basement. He stumbled around the room, clutching his face and screaming in pain, as I quickly began jumping from leg to leg, slicing each off as quickly as possible. Finally, he came crashing to the ground, mutilated spider legs surrounding us. Not wanting to spend another minute in the asylum, I grabbed the first aid kit and charged towards the door, hearing the creature's footsteps echoing behind me. I burst through the door, raced to the truck, threw the door open, and started the ignition, just as I saw the creature reach the front door.

He let out a menacing screech, then outstretched his arms as long, black, leather bat-like wings launched out of his back. I could see the plants around him wave in the breeze as he began to take flight. I slammed my foot down on the gas pedal, the tires screeching as the truck roared out of the parking lot, and drifting onto the gravel road that led towards town. I sat sternly, shifting as the machine began to speed down the road. 60-70-80-90 mph. I looked in the review mirror to find the creature charging towards the truck, then colliding with the roof making a loud "crash". Rumbling ripped across the roof of the cab, and an arm reached down and shot through the window, struggling to grasp me and drag me out. I drew my pistol from it's holster, and fired through the roof of the truck, the beast letting out yet another loud screech as I regained control of the wheel. We raced through town, the truck launching over hills and landing with the sounds of a roaring engine and springs echoing throughout. I leaned out of the window, then began firing repeatedly, the creature taking each shot through it's wings, and two or three penetrating it's chest. It lifted into the air, turning and flying back towards the asylum, almost as if it had given up, but I had refused to take any chances. I raced towards my bunker, the truck sliding to a halt in front of the entrance, and I scooped the first aid kit and enough of my supplies to last through the night and the next day before darting towards the cover, throwing it open, throwing my supplies into the hole, climbing in, slamming the cover behind me, and jumping to the ground. I collapsed against the wall and began panting. There was more going on in this town than just madmen running wild, something that raised the stakes for living in this town to drastic levels. The first aid kit clicked open at the press of the button sealing the box, then I found a needle and thread, and began stitching my wounds back together. I collapsed in the corner of the room on the cold, hard, concrete, feeling every muscle in my body ache.

Insanity Falls

This is intolerable. Only one man and we were still defeated. He even managed to take one of our own. I was the first to fish Mallard out of the pool of blood, and left his corpse in the corner of my office, waiting to decide whether or not I should have Jeremiah revive him. He was as traitorous as the thirteenth disciple, would have killed Bob before we could take him in, and would have left immediately after. If we brought him back, I'd have to enforce more discipline, take away more rights. I immediately got to work on the ones that remained. Each lined up awaiting punishment, all with fearful expressions and hidden loathing in their eyes. They hated me, but were too afraid to defend themselves. I had as much control as I needed, but they needed to be pushed harder. Standing tall, towering over them, supported by my spider legs, each peered up at me, waiting for punishment. I started with Jeremiah, throwing one leg behind his head and slamming him to the ground, then worked my way through BunnyMan Dave by flinging him through the glass window at the reception desk, and finished by striking Fantasia across the face, as she cluttered to the ground.

I spoke as I went on with their punishments, "YOU'RE ALL PATHETIC!" I grunted, striking each of them repeatedly. "ONE MAN, ONE MAN AND YOU STILL COULDN'T DO YOUR JOB! HOW HARD COULD THIS POSSIBLY BE?! YOU'RE ALL PSYCHOPATHS! MURDERERS! ACT LIKE IT! SHOW SOME TALENT IN YOUR PROFESSION!". Fantasia shivered, trying to lift herself off of the ground as she spoke.

"Wuh....we..." I slammed her head against the ground, her face cracking against the linoleum floor and echoing throughout the room.

"You....you what?" I said imitating her, while at the same time questioning what her excuse could possibly be.

"We tried.....He's good..." she continued.

"I don't care what his skill level is, you've all taken an immense amount of victims! 'He's good' is no excuse. YOU'RE SUPPOSED TO BE BETTER!"

They each lay barely conscious, staring at me out of the corners of their eyes, through necks that, at the moment, hurt too much to bend to look in any other direction. I stormed out of the room, rubbing one hand over my arm where the bullets had penetrated. As much as I hated to admit it, he WAS good. I knew why Lucifer wanted to recruit him. He had power and experience. More than any of us has ever had. I stepped into my office and sat down at my desk, then began to think. We'd need something better to bring him down. We'd need to be faster, stronger, quicker, and wittier than him. I lit a cigarette and stepped outside of my office. Each of my minions had already recovered enough to scamper out of the asylum and back into the world, fearing me more than the lunatics who now roam the ruins of Smithland. I decided to continue with my work, and came to the conclusion that he was unnaturally powerful, so we'd need to rely on the supernatural to bring him in.

I turned towards the stairs and began on my way down the long staircase, pass the basement and into two massive, heavy, wooden doors. The paneling around the doors was carved to bare the faces of demons, and those who now rot in hell. The door gave off a thick heat, hinting to what could be found on the other side. I shoved the door open and ventured down a long, vacant hallway that eventually branched off and opened up into the underworld, ending at a small plateau where one could stand and watch sinners fall to their fate, screaming and begging their gods for mercy.

At one side of the plateau sat a stairway, which led to a brimstone path that ran to the heavy front doors of my father's castle.

I followed this, and upon my arrival, was once again escorted by two guards to the throne room, where I found my father sitting in his throne and Na'amathe, sitting on his lap with her arms wrapped around his neck, both admiringly and seductively. I didn't want to ask for his help. I wanted to show that I had strength. I wanted to show that I had the power it takes to bring in Bob the Butcher, but this was the unfortunate conclusion that I was drawn to.

"My son. Have you brought our patron?", he asked, in his usual deep and powerful tone.

"No, father" I replied, "I.....Actually came to request your assistance."

"You need my help? One man was too much for the Anti-Christ and a band of murderous psychopaths to take in?" His fatherly tone had left, now becoming that of the furious businessman.

"Yes....Father, I..."

"Don't explain, you've already done enough. I thought the son of Satan would have more power over a mere mortal, but apparently I thought wrong.". He leaned over to one of his servants and spoke a hushed order.

"Father," I asked "What are your plans?"

"You need help. I'm giving you the best there is. I'm sending Legions with you. He can get the job done."

My heart sank. Even with my position in the underworld, I felt I had little power over Legions. He was powerful, maybe more powerful than me. I listened as the click clack of leather boots echoed down the hallway leading to the throne room. We all stood and waited, watching as the door, slowly swung open, revealing the figure of the man. But this was no man, this was a creature of hell and earth, born of pure hate fire, and raised of the darkest ashes of the underworld.

This was Legions. He stood with a long black trench coat encasing his body. Underneath he wore black dress pants, with black leather boots. His face was a pale white, and he smiled with an elongated mouth, baring sharp, jagged teeth. His nose was formatted like that of a snake's, limited to two narrow slits in the center of his face. His eyes were solid black beads, almost like marbles. He stood gazing around the room, waiting for his next command, breathing in and out with a whisper comparable to that of a snake's hiss.

"Legions", my father spoke out, "I am recruiting you to return to the surface world with my son. We have a project in need of your assistance, a bounty. Can I count on you?" His smile, impressively, seemed to grow wider as he focused his attention on my father, and nodded his head.

"It would be my pleasure, sire." he hissed.

"I felt the need to force my opinion. Anything involving Legions was sure to end badly. He didn't work for the underworld; he worked for himself and by his own rules. This would be completely out of our hands.

"Father, I.."

"You will leave now, and you will not disappoint me again."

He lit a cigar, and watched out his window as we left the room, and at that instant, we had returned back to the surface world. Upon our return, the others had gathered in front of us in a mediocre line, scattered back and forth similar to pieces on a checkerboard, but each stood at attention awaiting their next order.

"Alright guys, I know how things went last time, but I'm confident that, thanks to some heavy discipline, we won't have the same mistakes."

A tear streamed down Fantasia's face, seemingly in remembrance of who was in control, but I carried on. "Now, I wan..."

"I want each of you to sit back and let me take him." Legions interrupted. I stared at him, nerve bubbling up inside of me with my next question.

"Excuse me?" I asked, waiting to hear the same response. "Mr. Robert Elderson is mine." I stood face to face, putting all of my effort in as an intimidating person, but he stood, lacking any response to my tone. "Have you forgotten your place? You work for..." With that, he forced me to the ground by my throat, and with a flash, a snap echoed throughout the room, along with the tearing sound of flesh. I screamed out as he ripped away my arm, then, without hesitation, swung it, striking me across the face full force, and then threw it aside, then delivered a heavy blow with his boot, striking me in the chest.

He stood up and turned away, and with his back turned, replied "I work for your father, not for you."

I watched as he walked away, leaving the group and I together. I turned to them, waiting for the assistance that was sure to follow, but to my amazement, none was delivered. They only sat with blank stares, eyes focused on me.

"Well", I replied, becoming impatient "Who is going to help me up?!"

They all turned away and walked a path that faded into the distance, and I gritted my teeth and screamed out every name that came to mind.

"Cunt, fucker, bitch, traitor", but spoke to no one. They were already gone, and I had already lost control.

Bob the Butcher-Prey

It had been four days since the incident at the mental health facility, and since my return, I decided not to take any chances. I began upgrading security around my bunker. Working with welding and tools left over from an abandoned hardware store downtown, I was able to construct a metallic, hinged door that covered the entrance and exit of the bunker. It was made of a few thick sheets of metal, and had a crank on the inside that would allow it to lock shut. I was also able to recover supplies from other abandoned buildings around town. For example, I finally have a mattress, something more comfortable than the cold, hard ground to sleep on. I kept my new bed in the corner of the room, my puppet friend propped against the wall next to it. I also recovered a few books that would manage to keep me entertained while time passed by. Waiting for what, I was still unsure.

I kept a journal of each day that had passed, documenting everything from the conversations I would have with Smiles the puppet to the sounds of screaming lunatics, scratching and pounding at the door to get in. The door showed it's strength and I smiled with pride at my craftsmanship, finding sanctity in my dank, cold hole in the ground. That sanctity was ripped away with a painful intensity one night, however.

The night started off as usual. I sat on my mattress carrying on a conversation with Smiles. We'd laugh and make jokes about the poor fools that still roamed the streets, overly confident with their survival skills. As usual, then came the pounding of fists on the door to get in. We watched, together, as the door jiggled only slightly, under the pressure of bony fists, then, came a soft hissing sound, like a snake. The door stopped jiggling, and the screams echoing from the outside faded, leaving the only sound, the light hissing. Then, a heavy metallic sound that was comparable to construction girders being driven into the door. The door bounced heavily, street lights beginning to show through the cracks that were now forming, and bolts fell from the door, striking the ground with a "clank". We watched as, with one final strike, the door ripped off of it's hinges and dropped to the ground with a loud crash. I stared up through the entrance, to find no one there. I sat contemplating my next move, until I noticed the light bulb flicker, then shatter. The street lights showing through the opening gave my shadow life, and I stared at the concrete walls in curiosity.

Who was trying to break in? Who WAS able to break in? Before a second thought could come to mind, I began noticing humanoid shadows on the walls, first one, then another on a separate wall, and another on a different wall, each appearing with a new shadow until I was surrounded by at least twelve or thirteen. I stumbled back, as each shadow began to form together, into one, solid black mass which held the figure of a man. I stared at the face, as the darkness began to tear away, quite literally, like threads, revealing a grotesque row of teeth, dark eyes, and pale white skin leaking through underneath. I dove for my gun and opened fire, the bullet piercing the torso of the creature, creating a small gap through it's body. It still stood, staring at me. I fired twice more, each bullet penetrating the torso, and a thick black substance splashing to the ground with every strike, but still to no effect. Next, I grabbed my knife and began to charge, but before I could get within five feet, it bellowed out a heavy scream as an elongated arm swung out at me, striking me against the wall, stealing my breath and sending me gasping for air.

I struggled to sit up, and looked to my side, finding the ladder leading my way out of the room. I scrambled to my feet and began quickly pulling myself up the ladder, until I felt, once again, the tight grasp of a dark hand around my torso, dragging me to the ground with another heavy thud. I lost my breath again, and was struggling to gain control of my breathing, as the creature dove on top of me, pinning my arms and legs, preventing me from being able to move. Then, with one final act, raising a heavy hand with long black claws branching out at the finger tips, and pierced my chest, forcing it's fist straight back to my spine. I attempted to scream out in pain, but was only able to blubber, choking in my own blood. My vision as fading. Just before blacking out, I watched as another man, this one missing an arm and dressed in black with long black hair made his way down the ladder in a hurry. I recognized him as having the same face as the creature I fought at the sanitarium. He approached my body in a hurried manner, then scowled at the creature.

"What were you thinking?! We were supposed to take him back alive! Father will be furious!" He snapped, and at that instant, the creature turned, shot a hand through

the mans neck, and ripped out the lining
that incased it.

The man fell to the ground, clutching
his throat, then turned, walking away, finally
letting a few words leak from his jagged,
reptilian mouth.

"I don't give a shit." He said,
continuing on his way, and at that instant,
my vision had surrendered to solid darkness.

When I awoke, I was sitting at a black
meeting table in a dark room, at least it may
have been. The lack of light made the entire
setting appear to be one giant area, not
trapped in by four walls. My eyes darted
around the area, trying to make out shapes,
bodies, people, anything, but only to a lack
of success. A voice echoed from behind me.
A Dark voice with a tone that sounded
wrongfully soothing greeted me, and I
turned around to meet him, a tall man,
wearing a business suit. He had long black
hair, yellow eyes, and a black goatee. He

wore many rings on his hand, which became apparent as he shook his hand out to greet me.

"Robert Elderson, I presume.". He had a strong grip, numbing my hand as I shook it.

"Who are you?" I questioned, sorting through whether or not I should feel fearful.

"I go by many names. You may call be by one of my more common ones, and one that I'm sure you're familiar with. I'm Lucifer." I stumbled back from my chair at the sound of the name, and reached for the blade in my sheath, only finding that they had all been removed.

"Oh, Robert. Did you really expect to never end up here? You, of all people? As I recall, you carved the face off of a birthday clown at a children's birthday party about twenty years back? Which reminds me, I've got something for you, but you've got to help me first."

From one hand, launching out of the darkness, he tossed a figure onto the table that only became vivid when landing in front of me. It was my mask. I looked at him, still confused, still curious what had brought me into this situation.

"Why do you need me?" I asked, hesitant, fearing what his reply might be.

"Simple." He replied, "I need your handy work. From what I've observed, you've become quite the skilled killer over the years, and this is just what we're looking for, for a little expansion project that we have in store."

I remained silent. For years I had taken lives out of mercy. If I had accepted this proposition, I'd be killing for an entirely new reason, pure evil. He grew impatient waiting for a response, and continued.

"Come now, there must be something you want. I can give you anything in the world. Women? Money? Fame? Power? You name it."

I collected my thoughts, and found the answer I wanted. In a flash, I shot up, and swung a fist, striking him against the face. He took a step back, but then popped his neck, staring at me, his businessman smile fading to a scowl. I ran with as much intensity as I could force out, burrowing through solid walls of darkness, only being assisted by the occasional spot light of flame. I charged until I was out of breathe, and felt that Satan was far behind. I took a few steps forward, only to feel a solid mass ram against my calves, sending me backward, landing on a hospital bed, and, just as quickly, being secured by leather straps. A spotlight showed the face of Satan once more, his eyes growing an even more fiery yellow than before. He held out one hand, revealing on each fingertip, a different blade that stretched at least six inches off of the ring that held them on. He drew one blade across my chin, sending a steady flow of blood down my neck.

"Let's not do this the hard way, Robert." he stated, regaining his businessman composure. "There must be something you want. I'm willing to give you this, in exchange for your help. What is it that you want, Mr. Elderson?", he continued driving the blades across my face, leaving thin, blood dripping cuts along each part that the blades had touched. I rocked my head to the side, sending a wave of blood splashing off of my face, then looked him in the eyes with a scowl, knowing that there was only one thing that I could do.

"I want to get the hell out of Smithland", I said through my teeth. He grinned a sickening smile, then removed one strap, freeing one hand for a handshake.

"It appears we've found an agreement, Mr. Elderson. Pleasure doing business." I shook his hand, only being yanked closer as he sent one hand slashing across my throat. The pain was overwhelming, but with a flash the bed was gone and I was free from the leather straps.

I sat up, hands wrapped around my throat, finding no blood. My breathing had recovered. I looked around my room to find myself back in my bunker, the door still broken off the hinges and the light bulb still shattered, and now, a draft leaking in through the hole that lead to the surface. I climbed out through the hole, found my truck, creaked the door open, and plopped down into the driver's seat, exhausted. I closed my eyes, and just as quickly, fell asleep. I woke up the next day in a daze. Everything that had happened seemed to slip away like a dream. That is, until I sat up and noticed a small black package placed on the hood of the truck. On it, in red chicken scratch writing, it was marked "For Robert".

I tore open the package, and a sheet of black paper with more red chicken scratch writing was found inside, stating "Be at the asylum by noon." Underneath, I found my mask, in the same condition I left it in when it was confiscated by the officials at the hospital (which seemed odd, being that my mask has burned in an attempt to "rehabilitate" me). I took the letter seriously, and began preparing to return to the building of which I had thought that I had finally left behind. I prepared myself for the same ambush as before, arming myself with one bowie knife, one hunting knife, a collection of throwing knives, a hatchet, and two sig saur 240s. This time, if they tried to kill me, I'd take them first. Not only that, I'd cut off each of their heads and string them up above my bed, making lovely display pieces to fall asleep to. I checked the watch I had procured during one of my night raids of the neighborhood houses. 11:20 AM. I'd have plenty of time to eat, then be on my way.

I returned to the bunker, which appeared to have been rummaged through while I slept, and prepared the breakfast of my usual diet. Dry oatmeal and a bottle of water, then made my way out of the bunker, grabbed my mask from the box, and climbed into the cab of the truck. The engine roared to life, and I left, on my way to the asylum. The truck rolled into the parking lot at 11:53 and I took a few deep breaths before stepping out. I slipped my mask on in a simple movement. The instant the sole of my boot met the pavement; I dove into defense mode, ready for whatever Satan, his demons, or the asylum could throw at me. I carefully propped the front door open, sliding it just slightly forward, as to not reveal myself to anyone waiting in my room, but to my surprise, the door pulled forward on it's own, and standing on the other side of the door was Legions, grinning his usual face-wide grin, teeth gleaming in the sunlight.

"Robert, so nice of you to make it", he said with a hiss, grinning impossibly wider, "Please, join us.", he waved his arm over towards a group of three people, each peculiar in their own, psychotic ways.

He made all of the formal introductions, introducing me to each of these strange characters. David, or "Bunny man Dave" as they called him, was a tall man with a muscular build. He wore a brown, tattered, torn dress suit and an old, white bunny mask. Next was Jeremiah. He was a slender fellow with a thin face, sunken-in eyes, and long, scraggly black hair. He wore a black sweat shirt, dark jeans, and black boots. Last was the woman I had recognized from the basement, the woman who had licked the blood from my wounds. She had black, lifeless eyes, and erotic smile, long black hair, and stood completely nude. A simple diagnosis would show that she was clearly the nymphomaniac of the group. I'll have to admit; she did have a beautiful body with nice, perky breasts, and stood with excellent posture, not to mention how I admired her for being the only person in the room still capable of bearing a smile, without having it etched in through years of acts of evil. I felt I would blend well. I had recognized them as being patients at the asylum, more victims of the false, yet over-powering word of a medical professional.

I took my place with the group, and awaited orders from Legions, who introduced himself as the new leader of the group. I listened loosely as Legions explained how each night we'd separate into groups, he would go off on his own, while Fantasia and Jeremiah, and Bunny man Dave and I would team up, As seemingly normal procedure, he explained my partners condition and explained that we'd be targeting young adults. In a way, I admired Dave for targeting children. Taking them out at an early enough age would prevent them from ever having to experience the horrors of the world. The meeting had closed and each of us had gone our own ways, most leaving back to their own cells and various rooms around the building that they called home, while I went back to the cell that I had been kept in during operating hours. The television showed pure static, and, once more, I switched off the TV and laid in my bed, staring at the ceiling.

Everything about the room was the same. The same cracks lined the ceiling, the same dents from furious psychopaths' fists filled the walls. I closed my eyes and imagined the nurses bringing in my "medication". The pills that would slip me into drug induced comas that would allow them to pass me off as something that "wasn't their problem anymore". That day we moved everything that wasn't already stolen (being that the bunker no longer had a door to keep out the thieves), from my bunker into the asylum, my new home. The robbery was an unfortunate one. I did not have many things of value, but they did steal the one thing I cherished, my beloved companion, Smiles. I sighed a deep breath,

152

but decided to not let the casualty deter me from feeling comfortable in my new home. Soon after being settled in, I was given the grand tour of the building.

I saw every room and every corridor excluding the basement. As we passed by, the basement seemed dark, as if little electricity was provided to that part of the building. In fact, the light that led down the stairs flickered dimly, marking the lack of power generated to that part of the building. I marked this as having little relevance to the rest of the facility, and made myself at home. We went about what would become our normal routine. Carrying conversations with new acquaintances, wandering the many, long and maze-like halls of the asylum, and later that night, met for dinner in the cafeteria.

I had eaten a 'balanced diet' of oatmeal, and old distilled water for so long that I had forgotten what real food was like. Jeremiah showed his skill in the kitchen, preparing a steak dinner, with vegetables, mashed potatoes, and clean, filtered water to drink. It was delicious, a delicacy I haven't had in years. I finished dinner feeling immensely full, my appetite finally satisfied. I finished within minutes, the rest either scarfing down the meal like rabid dogs, or barely eating at all. Fantasia merely shuffled food around on her plate, not eating a bite. Rather, she seemed to keep her attention focused on me, but was discrete. I had only noticed that each time that I looked up from my plate, she was staring at me, and the instant I noticed, her eyes darted off to a different corner of the room. I had a moment to observe her expression. It wasn't flirtatious; it was a look of deep thought. I'd grow to learn her thoughts as time went on, but as of now, it had remained a mystery. Each of my other new acquaintances finished dinner, and afterwards, we did a full lock down on the facility, securing the gate outside to lock the psychopaths out of the asylum. The irony was too much.

Afterwards, we gathered in the social room

of the building, and sat together, some listening to crackled music rumbling over the old, outdated speakers that filled the building, others smoking cigarettes, but all keeping to themselves.

Once again, I caught Fantasia sending casual glances. We sat together for about four hours, until about 10:30 PM. At that time, each individual would slip away, returning to their cells and parts of the building for rest. I was one of the last to leave, but became drowsy and eventually returned for rest. I laid awake, unable to sleep, no matter how exhausted I was and happy to sleep in a safe haven, one much better than my hole in the ground. I had too much on my mind. My deal with the devil, how I'd eventually leave Smithland and return to the outside world, what was on Fantasia's mind throughout the day, and more importantly, why is this happening? Why are maniacs running the streets with no one to control them? Where are the police? Where is the fire department? The town had gone up in flames many times with no one but civilians to put out the fires. Why was it that we couldn't pick up any stations on the televisions, and why couldn't we pick up any stations on the radios? Earlier, we had to use cassettes to allow music to play throughout the building for this very reason. It was eerie....Disturbing....As if we had no contact with the rest of the world.

All of these thoughts twirled around my mind like a carousel of a headache. I decided to go for a walk and let my mind wander. I grabbed a flashlight and stepped out of my bedroom into the empty corridor, finding moonlight leaking through the windows, providing enough light to see my path. I made my way down the hallway, towards the main corridor, hearing the occasional snoring as I'd pass by each cell, and eventually ended up in the large corridor that would lead to different rooms in the facility. I followed down, then took a left, making my way into the library. The room was pitch black. I switched the flashlight on, and began making my way past the several columns of books, until I found a section that I felt appropriate. If I was going to get any rest tonight, I'd need to put my mind at ease, and to put my mind at ease, I'd need to study some history on the prison that entombed me. I began sorting through several old newspapers and binders marking the history of Smithland. I studied each decade, throwing myself deeper and deeper into confusion. Every article seemed...normal. Going back, it seemed like this was the perfect town. No crime rate, no murders, no burglaries. Every article was dedicated to irrelevant news; puppies for sale, achievements of local fishermen, achievements of local hunters. Even more peculiar, throughout the binders, there was no police record to be found. I sat back, clasping my hands over my face, trying to make sense of it all, when I heard a crash from the corner of the room.

I jumped up quick and spun around. Just beyond one of the aisles, a dark figure moved from book case to book case, eventually fading away. In my sense of security, I had left my knives back in my room. I braced myself to attack whoever the mysterious intruder was, raising my fists in fighting stance as I made my way through the library. I saw the brief figure of a humanoid shape dart through a doorway and out of the room. I stood up, letting my guard down, even more confused about who had been watching me, only to feel a burst of energy coming from behind me. I landed flat on my stomach, then rolled over onto my back as quickly as possible, only to feel someone pounce on top of me. I grabbed the flashlight, then shined the light above me. It was Fantasia, once again, fully nude, straddling my torso. Her hands ran down my chest, as her beautiful eyes met mine.

"What do you think you're doing?" she said in a sensual voice.

"I...I was doing some reading...Why are you..."

"I was following you. I won't lie, from the moment I saw you, I've been thinking about how much I wanted to take you into my bedroom and go crazy.....well, crazier."

She smiled, and leaned close, her breasts dangling forward. "What do you say, cowboy? You wanna go for a ride?"

"I don't think I....I couldn't...It's not right...You're..."

"What? Crazy? You know as well as I do that everything those doctors scribble into those books is a lie. So I'm a bit flirty. Is that going to kill anyone? Now come on, babe. I recognize you, I know your past, and I know how long it's been since you were with a woman. Are you really going to tell me you don't miss this?"

She grabbed my hands and placed them over hear breasts. I bit my lip. She was right. I hadn't been with a woman since my

wife was still alive. I gave in. I sat up, gently
laying her to her back, and kissed her lips,
she groaned as our lips touched. She opened
her mouth, and I opened mine, the wet
smacking sound carrying throughout the
room. I picked her up and carried her down
the hallway and into my cell, where I placed
her onto my bed, then began pulling off my
shirt. She stood up from the bed, wrapping
her arms around me, turning me towards
the bed now, and pushing me down. I
landed with a bounce, and she began pulling
off my pants, next, working at my boxers
with her teeth. Within minutes, we were
both completely nude, and she lay beneath
me, as I slowly worked my way from kissing
her lips, to kissing her neck, to kissing her
breasts, to her stomach, as I gently
massaged her pussy. I kissed the rim, just
before she gently rolled me onto my back,
crawled atop, and strattled me. She began
launching herself up and down on my dick,
grabbing her breasts as she did, groaning in
pleasure. As I continued thrusting, I pulled
her forward, and began kissing her once

more, my fingers trailing down her shoulder blades, and eventually meeting the base of her spine. I began thrusting harder, and she groaned louder, reaching the point of orgasm, as did I, as I came into her. She sighed, sweat running down her face, then leaned forward, laying next to me. She placed her head onto my chest, and I wrapped my arm around her waist, as we both panted, trying to catch our breathe. After a few minutes, we were able to recollect ourselves, and I was finally able to rest easy, as did she, who had nodded off as I held her close. I closed my eyes, and dazed into the most comforting slumber I had felt in years.

The next morning we woke up about the same time. Fantasia's head was still nested on my chest, and I leaned forward to kiss her forehead.

"Good morning, babe." I said, in a harmonic voice.

She looked up at me, laughed, and a shock of disappointment blew over me. "Babe? You're kidding, right?"

I frowned, "No...I thought..."

"Don't tell me you took that for anything more than a one night stand. That's all that this was. We're not suddenly boyfriend and girlfriend after one night of sex."

She cracked a smirk, showing that she was holding in laughter. I looked away. My heart sunk. I felt empty inside. I thought that I had found some source of happiness in this hell I've been entombed in for so long. Apparently she saw through my silence and saw my pain. She sat up and kissed me on the cheek.

"You're different though. Don't be surprised if we do this more than a few times a week."

She smiled, showing her beautiful white teeth, combed her hair back over her shoulders, and made her way out of my cell. I felt a little more at ease, but wanted much more than just a sexual partner. I wanted a connection with someone, someone like her. I sat up and sighed, setting the sad, sad thought away from my mind, knowing that eventually this could become something, and slipped my pants and a white tank top on. I ran my fingers across my prickled, shaven head, stood up, slipped my boots on, and went out into the main corridor to join the rest. I joined Jeremiah, who was lounging on the couch, still in his bed clothes, sitting shirtless and wearing black sweat pants. I joined his line of vision, focusing on the area his eyes were directed in. He was watching Fantasia, who was off with Legions, laughing and brushing her arm up and down his shoulder. He remained quiet, until finally, he commented, bringing the opening of our conversation to a crude topic.

"You know not to take her too seriously, right?" I sat up at attention at the sound of this.

"What are you talking about?"

I wondered how he knew about us last night, and I wondered if Fantasia was less worthy of the trust I was putting in her.

"Oh please. You two were loud last night. I know what happened. We all know. She's a nymphomaniac and a psychotic. She'll lie and cheat to get what she wants, which usually ends in sex."

I scowled at the sound of this. I found it distasteful. Little had I known, I had already developed affection for the girl.

"You shouldn't say something like that about her." My voice deepening as my temper began to rise.

"Whatever. I'm just warning you, man. You're with us now. You're family. I thought I should warn you before you became too involved. She tried pulling the same thing with me."

The conversation ended there, and we both remained silent, until Jeremiah stood up and returned to the kitchen, where he'd prepare breakfast: omelets, bacon and sausage, clean water. Once again, a better meal than I've been able to eat in years. I sat with my new companion and David, while Jeremiah and I watched across the lunch room at Fantasia and Legions. They were eating together, she was smiling and laughing as he'd make crude jokes, and eventually began running his hand along her smooth leg. She smiled and welcomed it, as we both scoffed in disgust. We decided to focus our attention elsewhere.

"You know, tonight we'll be going on our first slaughter. You looking forward to it?"

I swallowed a mouth full of bacon, then replied "Yes. I've never actually killed in a group before. It'll be a different experience, I trust?"

"Like none other. We're all very productive when it comes to the murder game. We usually accomplish a lot by the time the night's over.",

"Not that we need a group to commit a good genocide.". He smiled at the joke, as did I, then I looked up at Dave.

"What's your plan? Are you looking forward to it?". He remained silent, leaving the question in the air. Jeremiah butted in, answering for Dave.

"He's looking forward to it. Only time I ever see the guy happy. He won't answer you if you ask him, though. Hasn't talked since they brought him here. He started this whole I'll never talk for a doctor, and I'll never let them evaluate me like the other poor fucker's here' act, and has been sticking with it ever since."

This gave me even more of an admiration for Dave. Now he was the person who would take the life of a human at an early age, before they could experience the cruelty of the world, and felt that he would never need to present an explanation for his actions. We finished our breakfasts, and went about our days, eagerly counting down the hours until 8:00 PM. At that time, we all met in the main corridor where Legions would review the plans for the night. Once again, he'd go off on his own, Jeremiah would go with Fantasia, and Bunny man Dave and I would go together. We'd start at the North, East, and West ends of the town, and, Legions, confident with himself, would take both South and West. We'd storm each house, slaughtering the residents inside and killing anyone we'd cross out on the streets. We prepared ourselves with walkie talkies and all of the necessary weaponry; guns, knives, chainsaws, explosives, and we'd met with our team members. I stood with Dave, he, of course, remaining perfectly quiet the entire time. I couldn't help but let my eyes wander around the room awaiting the "roll out" signal.

My eyes landed on Fantasia and Jeremiah. Jeremiah seemed cold to Fantasia, completely unwilling to talk to her, and I found Fantasia, once again shooting casual glances in my direction. I was lost in my thoughts, only to snap back in at the sound of Legion's snake-like voice echoing "Let's go, people!"

We each gathered into comfortable positions in my truck, and I shifted into drive, the death carrying machine rolling through the parking lot, carrying each of us to our drop off points. Legions, Fantasia, and Dave all took the back seat while Jeremiah and I sat in the front together. Being that the asylum was on the west part of town, Legions was dropped off first. Next, we worked our way into the North part of town, where Fantasia and Jeremiah were dropped off. Then finally, the truck rolled to stop on the East end of town, where Dave and I had stepped out. The streets were rampant with wild men, and I took no hesitation to draw my firearms and begin gunning them dead. Each began to run, but as my bullets surfaced through their cranium, they'd each collapse, almost doing a front flip. I made my way to the first house, a large, Victorian two story house, then tricked the lock and opened the door, as to not wake it's residents.

I began dousing each room in gasoline starting with the living room, then working my way to the bed rooms. In each bed lay a different family member, sleeping too heavily to sense my presence. I soaked the beds in fuel, then retreated to the kitchen, struck the lighter, leaned down to light the trail, then watched the flames erupt. I stepped back and watched as a fiery red glow encased the house and screams of the family echoed inside. I craved the sound of it, and I wanted more. Luckily, I had many more houses to stop by, so I carried on, leaving the house to burn. At the next house, I kicked the door in, as to strike fear into it's inhabitants. I held my gun at ready aim as each member began running down the hallway, then sliding to a halt as soon as they saw me. One by one they dropped dead as bullets erupted through their skulls. I stepped back, then turned towards the other side of the street and listened to the screams that carried from David's symphony of slaughter. I smiled, my lust for blood being satisfied, then continued onto the next house, after once more returning to the truck to retrieve a chainsaw. I kicked the door open, then began walking through each room of the house, revving the engine to bring liveliness to the people inside, but to no avail. No reaction. There was no one to be found. I made my way through each room of the house, the bedroom being the last room I'd check.

As I stepped in, my jaw dropped. I stumbled back, dropping the chainsaw to stare at what I had found. Inside was the corpse of a man, who seemed to have bled to death, but not before leaving a message. In large lettering on the wall at the end of the room were the words "PLEASE TAKE IT AWAY!" scrawled in thick blood. I examined the room more to find Smiles sitting at the head of the corpse, wearing his usual, unnaturally disturbing smile. I picked him up, and wiped off the blood that stained his costume the best I could, then retrieved him from the house with me. I left the puppet in the cab of the truck, and continued with the slaughter until we got the "Return to base" call from Legions.

We had covered a total of ten houses together, the rest pulling in similar numbers that ranged from five to twelve. We'd circled around at each of the pick-up points taking what had become our usual positions on the truck. Jeremiah inspected the streets, his eyes watching burning houses and corpses in the streets, until eventually his eyes returned to the inside of the cab of the truck, where he happened upon Smiles.

"What's this?" he asked in a friendly tone.

"That's Smiles. I had him a while ago. Someone stole him from me. I found him tonight."

"I trust you sliced him up for it?"

"No, he beat me to it.". Jeremiah gave a smile, showing that he was enthused by the results our endeavor had brought us.

As soon as we arrived back at the asylum, we each walked the ground searching for intruders, then went through the lock down process, later to meet in the main corridor to meet for review. Legions walked down the line with a clipboard and pen, jotting down the kill ratio for each of us. The results were thirty six kills in three hours. Not bad. In no time, we'd have the town completely cleared out. Legions gave the okay to leave, and at that, many of us returned to the showers to wash up, then went off to our cells for rest. I left Smiles propped against the wall at the far corner from my bed and had just barely laid down before Fantasia welcomed herself in.

"Hey you." she said, smiling and climbing on top of me.

"Hey." I replied oddly, feeling that I knew her intentions.

"You have fun tonight?"

"Yes."

Her smiled dropped to a frown. "What's wrong?"

"Nothing."

Her eyes grew large, then replied with a huff "Come on, tell me. What did I do?"

"I talked to Jeremiah. I know what you're after. I know what you're like. The sex is great, but I've been waiting for this too long to play this kind of game. I'm not in this just for the sex."

"Robert, we just met and..."

"And what?" I interrupted. "Do you really have room to talk? I've seen you. All of these casual glances. You want more too. Don't deny yourself of that. It doesn't matter how long I've known you or you've known me, we're each looking for the same thing, happiness in this god damn prison of a town, and I don't think we're going to find it anywhere else. So if you want to play, then fine. but get the fuck out and don't play with me." I sat down on the bed and she sat down with me.

"Robert...You're different. I've known this about you since I first saw you in the basement. It's in your eyes. There's something familiar there. Maybe someone I had lost a while back. I think you remind me of him..." We both looked at each other, our eyes meeting.

"Remind you of who?" I asked.

"My fiancé, his name was Richard. He was a lot like you. Strong minded, but not above helping others. He even looked like you too. He was in good shape, had the same jaw line, and would always look at me with that same look you're giving me now. I haven't seen it in years. Before it was all about the sex, now...I don't know. Maybe there is something more." I turned my head away to think, then looked back at her.

"This is you, isn't it? The real you. When you're not on some outrageous quest for sex, you can connect with a person, even me. No one has done that since my wife was

175

around." Her eyes left mine, then followed to the corner of the room.

"Can we make this work, or are we just trying to replace someone we loved?" I placed my hand against her cheek, pulling gently until her eyes met mine once more.

"I think we need to try. I think we both want to be happy, and we might be able to fill that gap in each other's lives. And you?"

"I think you're right.". We smiled at each other, then leaned back in the bed together, turning so that each of our heads would land on the pillow, then cuddled.

We didn't have sex that night. We just held each other, enjoying each other's company and talking, learning more about each other, and liking everything new we had learned. Eventually, she drifted off to sleep. I, however, was unable to sleep. I laid for what seemed like hours, waiting for my eyelids to eventually become heavy and slide shut on their own, but to my dismay, that time never came. Thoughts flowed through my mind like a hornets nest. Mainly, concern over what I had found in the library. The thought of what Smithland was, left me unnerved. I carefully slid away from Fantasia as to not wake her, grabbed a flashlight, and made my way back into the hallways.

I made my way down the hallway, an echo carrying with every step. Once again, I heard the somber sound of snoring carrying from each cell as I passed by, the walk seemingly as casual as the night before until I made the turn into the main corridor. I watched as a large black figure bolted across the corridor. I charged towards the sight, both confused about what the creature might be and concerned with who had invaded our home. I slid as I made the turn down the hallway that the creature had followed, and once again, saw the bare outline flow at an angle into another series of hallways, I charged, sliding around every turn like a baseball player might to a base, and eventually came to a halt when I found that the creature had followed down the wide stairwell and into the basement. I stood watching, considering the casualties I could run into by going into the basement, unarmed and unprepared, and eventually decided to return to my cell, grab a few weapons, and follow the stairs down and confront whatever it was I had seen, but before I could take a step back, the hanging light above, flickering and barely illuminating the area revealed a long dark, black tentacle launching up the stairwell and wrapping around my leg.

I felt a heavy tug, sending me to my back, my skull colliding against the floor upon impact. I gripped the back of my head in pain, then felt my body take flight down the stairwell, the light flashing away as quick as lightning. I felt the heavy swings as the tentacle would force sharp turns around corners, and eventually raising higher off the ground, then twirling in a position that left me hanging upside down, the blood from my head dripping down and making a small puddle on the floor. For a moment, there was no light, until the luminescent flicker of a television revealed the rest of the room and the face of my attacker. He had long, black, scraggly hair and gray eyes. He had an unshaven face, and lips that never stayed in position, as he was always mumbling. He was missing one arm, and in it's place hung long, black, thread like strands that would drip a disgusting yellowish brown substance. The tentacle holding me was one of many that were projected out of his back. I recognized this character as the man who attacked me during my first trip back to this asylum. I believe the others called him "Ben". I watched as he made his way back and forth across the room, pacing back and forth, mumbling in a rushed voice, occasionally randomly raising in volume and pitch.

"I...It's you!", he finally turned towards me and said.

I scowled, puzzled, yet furious that I had been attacked and not given a chance to defend myself.

"Yes, yes it's me. And you're Ben, I presume. What's the matter? Had to make sure I didn't see you coming? Didn't want to get your ass kicked again?"

"NO! NO NO NO NO NO! HA! I'M WARNING YOU! OF THINGS TO COME! THINGS TO COME! YOU LAUGH! YOU INSANE BASTARD! YOU DON'T KNOW!"

He had clearly gone insane since the last I had seen him, so much to the point that he could barely speak. I'd have to listen carefully to understand anything he said.

"What don't I know?", I asked, still confused.

"NOOOOOOO! I WON'T TELL! I SHAN'T! I CAN'T! I WON'T!" he grinned, revealing a row of jagged teeth.

"TELL ME DAMN IT! TELL ME OR PUT ME DOWN!". He chuckled a sickening, wheezy laugh, and with a flick, tossed me against the wall, my body impacting with a heavy "THUD", then once again I felt the pressure as another tentacle pounded me into the ground.

"HAHAHA, you! You wanna play a game? I'll tell you, but you've gotta play first! And no cheating! I hate cheaters! You won't like what happens to the cheaters!" He sunk his tentacle heavier on my torso, restricting my breathing.

I had no other choice, so with a strained voice, I replied "Yes."

He grinned wildly, then rubbed his chin, "Yes! Yes! A game! You'll love this game!"

"What's the game, Ben?" I replied, growing impatient.

"Okay, the rules of the game are I have to tell you a secret. After I tell you the secret, you die!"

I gritted my teeth. Once again, Ben was taking the unfair advantage. I had no means of defending myself, and he was ready to threaten my life, but, if he knew what I had hoped he'd known, then I'd take the secret and after, find a way to work my way out of his grip and kill him.

"Alright Ben, sounds fair. Tell me your secret." He drew me closer as to whisper in my ear, and as he drug me closer, it was revealed through a wide smile that blood dripped from his teeth and gums, which were broken, scared, and cut.

He drew me near enough that he could whisper in my ear, then, fluctuating randomly in tone and volume, forced the attempted whispered words, "The town is alive!!!!".

At that, he threw me across the room, my body crashing into old filing cabinets and office chairs. I rolled onto my back quick enough to watch the tip of a pointed tentacle jetting towards me, then rolled to the side just in time, the tentacle colliding with the wall. Quickly, my eyes darted around the room for a tool of self-defense, and found an ax pinned in the corner of the room. I darted for it, dodging tentacles along my path, listening to Ben's frustrated grumbles. In a flash, I grabbed the axe, took a swift step aside, dodging one more tentacle, then grabbed the handle and with all of my strength, hacked the axe down against the tentacle, severing it. Ben screamed out in pain, focusing on the missing tentacle, and, making sure to use this distraction to my advantage, I charged at him, and, once reaching him, made a swift punch to his face, then jabbed him in his bony gut with the handle of the axe. He gripped his gut with both arms, and at that, I made my way behind him, then pinned his neck between the handle of the ax and the ax itself. He began choking and begging me to stop, but I ignored his pleas, determined to get the answers I was in search of.

"I WANT ANSWERS, DAMN IT!", I growled.

"What?! What do you want to know?!" He pleaded.

"TELL ME WHAT YOU MEANT! WHAT DO YOU MEAN "THE TOWN IS ALIVE?!"

"Let me go!", I grabbed harder, forcing the corner of the axe and handle deeper into his throat.

"Fine! Okay! Okay! This town...It's different....It lives, it breathes, and it picks and chooses between the people that can come here, but none can leave."

"Why do you talk about it like that? It can't be alive, it's just a-"

"This town! This town! This town is a gateway, dearie! The gateway lives! It breathes! It controls us!"

None of it made any sense, but then, nothing in Smithland made sense lately. I lightened my grip on the axe, sending him collapsing to the floor. He began to cry, letting out heavy sobs, that stained the dirt on his cheeks a darker color, then turned towards me.

"I spoke too much! Kill me! Damn it, Kill me!"

Before, I had killed because I took pity. This creature was filth, and for that very reason, I chose to let him suffer. I turned, dropping the ax to the ground and making my way out of the basement, when I heard the sound of a demons temper boil.

He began with a growl, then speaking through his teeth, snapped "YOU SON OF A WHORE!"

I listened and heard the grinding of the ax as it lifted off of the floor and heard sound of the tapping bare feet running across a concrete floor. I turned to watch as he neared me, and, at the spur of the moment, shot one leg up, striking him in the face with my boot and sending him crashing to the ground, the ax sliding across the room. "Don't let me catch you outside of this basement again." I ordered, and watched as he held his hands away from his face, blood and tears dripping down as he began to cry again. I made my way over to the ax, kicked it off of the ground and into my hand, and made my way back up the stairs, back through the corridor, and back to my cell, locking the door behind me, then crawled into bed, wrapping my arms around Fantasia's waist as I drifted off to sleep.

The next day I woke up to find that Fantasia had woken up before me, and had already left the room. I rubbed my eyes and let out a yawn before slipping into a white tank top, dark jeans, and my boots. I walked out to join the others to an astonishing sight. There, chatting with my new acquaintances stood Fantasia. A different Fantasia. A more respectable Fantasia. This Fantasia no longer presented herself in the nude or made sex her main objective. In fact, this Fantasia was wearing clothes! She wore a black tank top with dark jeans and leather boots. Her hair was back in a ponytail. Around her neck she wore a small necklace, and make up painted her face so beautifully, it looked like it should belong in an art museum.

She turned to face me, smiled, then greeted me with a hug, and in a pleasant tone, said "Good morning, Robert".

I hugged her back. "Good morning Fantasia....You look a bit different."

"Do you like it? Early this morning I borrowed your truck and made a few stops. Wasn't easy to get all of the supplies, but I should have plenty to last for a while."

Her new sense of self-respect showed as a definite note, and I was happy to see her like this. I could tell that she agreed with me on what we had discussed the previous night, and she did want to take our quest for happiness seriously.

"Should we go eat breakfast?" she asked, revealing a glamorous smile.

She took my hand, and led me to the cafeteria, where the three of us, Dave, Fantasia, and I, and after serving breakfast, Jeremiah sat together. She seemed more social and was swept up in a conversation with Jeremiah about the events that had taken place during our night raids. It was a conversation I would have enjoyed being a part of, but was too distracted. Across the cafeteria sat Legions, staring with a baron expression, anger seemingly hidden behind his eyes. The day went on, and I felt an overwhelming joy, feeling that I had finally connected with someone as I spent the day with Fantasia, and not a moment too soon. Over the past couple of nights, we had continued our expansion far enough to the point that we had one final sweep of the last neighborhood in town, then we were done. We had spent the day discussing what we were going to do with our lives as soon as we were set free from Smithland. Fantasia was putting heavy consideration into going back to school and getting her law degree. I wasn't entirely sure on what I would do yet. I had been trapped in confinement for the past thirty years, and I had never thought about anything other than escaping. Funny, when you're in those situations, you never think that far ahead. I knew one thing for sure though, and that was that I'd want to keep living with Fantasia. It wouldn't be anything extreme, really. We might live in the same apartment building, right across from the street of each other, or, maybe even in the same house or same apartment. I liked having her near me, and in the end, that's how I wanted it to stay.

Later that day, at least a few hours before leaving out to do our final sweep of the town, Fantasia and I sat outside, cuddled together, leaning against a tree and watching the sun slowly go down over the forest. Wind blew through the tall grass, sending it waving in the breeze, as did it hear long hair, rippling like tides at sea. She peered up at me through her hair, her beautiful eyes, now revealed to be a soft blue color, met mine, and I stared back, wearing a comforting smile. "I can't believe it's almost over." She said, sighing and looking back into the sunset.

"I know", I replied, "It's been years since any of us have been outside of the borders of this town. Starting tonight, we're free."

"What should we do when we get out there?", she asked, still staring off into the sunset.

"Well....We've been here for so long. Maybe we can change our names and go back to society. Maybe you could go back to school to be a lawyer like you wanted."

"And what about you?'. She glanced up at me, once again through her flowing black hair. I continued to watch the wind rustle along the trees and grass as I thought.

"I'm not sure. It's been a long road. I'm sure I'll come up with a plan as soon as we get out."

"We'll need a plan. We'll need to make sure Robert Jr. is well taken care of. He'll need a good school, a good home...", she continued staring at me, a smile growing wider across her face as I glanced down at her.

"Robert Jr.? You mean..."

"Yes, I'm pregnant!". She sat up and
threw her arms around my neck, as I
wrapped my hands around her waist, then
held her close, continuing the conversation
with excitement in my voice.

"When did this happen?"

"Remember a few nights ago? The
night we first had sex? I did a pregnancy test
the next day, and it came up positive!"

"So I'm going to be a father.", I
pressed my forehead against hers, smiling,
feeling contempt with something I thought I
would never see again, something I had too
easily thrown away years earlier.

She smiled, showing beautiful white
teeth, then with a breathe and a sweet, soft
kiss on my lips, replied "The best father a kid
could ask for."

We cuddled once more, relaxing under the tree for hours, wishing we could spend years just holding each other, but after those hours had passed, Legion's voice echoed over the speaker phone, beckoning all of us to the main hall of the building, and, with that, we helped each other up off the ground, then walked to the main hall, where we stood together, awaiting orders.

"Alright people, tonight will be our last night as a group. After this, you're all free to go. I want to congratulate you all on making it this far, and inform you of what a pleasure it has been working with you all. Thanks to your hard work, this project has gone by smoothly and without error. My only request is that we all meet back together before leaving the town for the night, this way each of us has a ride to the next town, then off to where ever the world takes us. Once again, we'll be dividing the group as follows: Robert will be with Bunny man Dave, Jeremiah will be with Fantasia, and I will be going alone."

"Actually", said Fantasia, butting in, "Robert and I were wondering if we could go together, and Jeremiah and Bunny man Dave could partner up."

Legions shot a scowl at me, then turned towards Fantasia, and scornfully replied "Yes...I suppose this once it's fine. But stay focused." Jeremiah patted me on the back, as if saying "congratulations", and I gave a quick smile back, before returning to attention.

At Legion's order, each of us left the building and took our rightful seats in the truck, this time Fantasia sitting in the front with me, while Dave, Jeremiah, and Legions sat in back. We began at the corners of each city block, slowly working our way in. Instead of separating as Dave and I had previously, Fantasia and I decided to stay together and team up, being that a few of the households on this street had families with as many as six members. I was quick with my slayings, though distracted by Fantasia's work. It was something I never had the ability to observe before. She'd start by waking the man and adult youth of each household, sensually coaxing them down the hallway towards me, where I'd generally be waiting with a knife, an ax, and at the last house, a chainsaw. Fantasia's work was a thing of beauty. It was graceful yet deceiving. She reminded me of a siren in olden folklore. At our last house, she broke routine. She approached the bedroom, where a man and his wife slept, pulled two knives out of sheaths that were held at her hips, then carefully and silently, slid up between the sleeping sheep. As she arrived at the top of the covers, she sat up, her back resting against the headboard of the bed. She placed the tips of each blade at the throats of her victims, then began to sing melodically and smoothly, slowly disrupting the man and woman from their sleep. Their eyes slowly drew open, as if feeling the presence of innocence, and then, feeling the pressure of the blade, and finding the stranger in their bed, began to panic. At this instant, Fantasia drew the knives across their throats, sending waves over her face as the gurgled sound of the couple drowning in their blood filled the room.

Fantasia sat up higher, then stepped over the man and out of the bed, then approached me, a smile spread across her face. She then held up one finger, soaked in blood, and softly brushed it onto my nose, before throwing her arms around my neck and kissing me deeply. I wrapped my arms around her waist, returning with deep passion, then scooped her into my arms, leaving the house, and approaching the truck, leaving Smithland, finally, once and for all. This time, instead of needing to do the usual pick up, each member of the group met in the center of the neighborhood block, then took our usual positions in the truck. An air of excitement filled all within, ready to begin our new life outside of this prison. I turned to Jeremiah, Legions, and Dave, wearing a broad smile over my face.

"Everyone ready to finally return to freedom?!"

"HELL YEAH!", Jeremiah replied, throwing a fist up in the air in excitement.

Dave nodded, and Legions maintained his usual chilling smile. I turned to face Fantasia, who glanced at me with a smile, then rested her hand over mine, as I shifted into drive. We exited the neighborhood and began on the main road leaving town. We each watched eagerly as the truck rumbled past the road sign stating "Now leaving Smithland". The next town was twenty miles away, and from there, we'd each go our own separate ways. The truck rumbled on for hours, coursing down the tree-lined road, and we had all grown tired. I, myself, was fighting to keep my eye lids open, until the thin outline of a town began to appear at the end of the road. We had finally reached Cumberland.

"Alright everyone, we've reached Cumberland! Get ready for the sweet taste of freedom!" Excitement filled the cab of the truck at the sound of my announcement, but as we reached the road sign, our hearts sank. I heard Fantasia choke holding back tears.

"DAMN IT!" Jeremiah growled, driving a fist into the seat in front of him.

The truck came to a screeching halt at a sight of madness. There, in front of the truck, stood a large metallic road sign, reading "Now Entering Smithland!" A cackle echoed from the back seat, and with a few moments notice, it became clear that Legions was getting a thrill out of our displeasure.

"GET OUT OF THE TRUCK!" I demanded, meeting Legions back on the road with Dave, Fantasia, and Jeremiah at my side.

"WHAT THE FUCK IS GOING ON?!", I questioned, and clenched my teeth as his sick grin stretched across his face.

"You fools. You can never leave. The road you're standing on is Lucifer's, along with the town that it leads to. It's his now, and he has all say in whether or not you can leave. And, I'm afraid, he's become quite fond of you. For reasons I quite easily understand." He said, throwing an arm around Fantasia's waste and letting his black forked tongue curve along her jaw line and across her cheek.

At that point I snapped. In a fit of rage I charged for him, and drove my fist across his face with as much force as I could, the loud crack echoing between the trees. He laughed once more, then glanced at me with a wide, sadistic grin.

"You always were the strong minded one Bob, but not strong enough. Good luck from here on out. You're going to need it."

199

With that, flames rose out of the ground encasing his body in a whirlpool, then, just as quickly as they appeared, they sank back into the ground, taking Legions with them.

We stared at the scorch marks on the ground left by the flames for minutes, the silence to be broken by Fantasia's questioning.

"What do we do now?" She asked, fear showing in her eyes. I rubbed my brow, at a loss of words.

"We go back to the asylum. We go back and we think of a new plan."

With that, and many words left unspoken by the group, we each climbed back into the truck which roared, making its way down the main road back to the asylum. I turned into the parking lot and the truck halted with a skid, signaling each of its passengers to step out and enter the asylum. Upon entry, we each divided up, retreating to our cells. Fantasia took her place in our room, laying arms wrapped around her knees as tears began to stream down her face. I joined her, holding her in my arms and wiping away her tears.

"It'll be okay babe, I promise."

"You can't promise that. Legions did and look where it got us! We'll never get out of here."

I felt a chilling feeling grow over my heart, and I felt sadness, not for me, but for her. I couldn't stand to see her in this much pain.

"I promise you, with all of my heart, I will find a way for us to get out of here." She sniffled, then looked into my eyes through droplets of tears, still forming. I wiped them away, then kissed her forehead.

"Get some rest, sweet heart." With that, she curled into bed, and I took my place with her, holding her in my arms, cuddling her.

After a long day, all that any of us had wanted was sleep. After only an hour, we had both dozed off. After a few hours had passed by, we were startled awake to the sounds of screaming, echoing throughout the building. It was a blood curdling scream, one that a person could only make when experiencing intense pain. Fantasia and I shot out of bed, and met Dave and Jeremiah in the hallway, as we each charged through the asylum, following our ears to the basement. Our footsteps rained down the metallic staircase and the light above flickered wildly. Jeremiah and I were the first to shoot around the corner, only to stumble back at what we had seen. There, in the center of the room, lay Ben, screaming in agony. On top, stood, who I believe was named Mallard, a fellow I had killed in a fight during my first return back to the asylum. Mallard was different in many ways, instead of speaking fluently, he hissed, like a snake might. His eyes were a smoky gray color. In his hands, he held bits of flesh ripped from Ben's severely mangled torso. He leapt to his feet at the sight of us, and let out a vicious snarl, then, without hesitation, lunged for me. In a flash, I ripped my gun out of it's holster and shot him three times as he soared through the air, sending him to the ground with a meaty "thud".

His body twitched and convulsed, as we gathered around to stare at him. I looked up at Jeremiah from under my brow, and with a tone of complete seriousness, asked "Jeremiah, what was the ritual we were taking part in? Why were we killing all of these people?"

He stared back at me, fear showing in his eyes, unwilling to speak. "DAMN IT! ANSWER ME!"

"I..." he began to spoke, but at that instant, the sounds of shattered glass carried from the main corridor of the building, followed by the sounds of several wildly screaming madmen.

As quickly as we could, we charged up the stairs and into the main corridor, to find twelve of our victims sprinting towards us. We each braced ourselves as they charged at us, ready to fight, knives and guns in hand. I took the first of them, firing at as many as possible, yet finding little success, they each carried on until their sixth or seventh shots. Behind me stood Jeremiah, Fantasia, and Dave, fighting by knives, slicing their way through the crowd of stampeding victims. I had just cleared my way through my targets, and turned to help Jeremiah, Fantasia, and Dave, but a moment too late. As I turned around the earth shattering scream of a woman in pain filled the air. Upon examination, I found that Fantasia had been attacked, a large bite taken out of her neck.

"NO!" I screamed, driving a fist across the jaw of her attacker with the speed of bullets.

He crashed to the ground, his jaw snapped away from the rest of his skull, and neck broken. I scooped Fantasia into my arms and directed the others to the truck. Jeremiah sat in the back with a first aid kit dressing Fantasia's wounds, while Dave sat in front, shot gun in hand and braced for the worst as I switched the ignition and the truck roared into gear. I slammed my foot down heavily on the accelerator, sending the truck ripping through the fence, and into a street filled with armies of victims we had killed.

"DAMN IT JEREMIAH! TELL ME WHAT'S GOING ON!" I shouted as the truck creamed through waves of the undead, torso's snapping in half at the cattle guard at the front of the truck, sending severed limbs bouncing off of the windshield.

"I'VE STUDIED EVENTS LIKE THESE! USUALLY HAPPENS IN PREPERATION FOR EITHER AN APOCALYPSE OR A GREAT WAR! THESE ARE LUCIFER'S ARMIES! WE WERE KILLING TO GIVE DEMONS EMBODIMENTS!"

"FIGURES", I replied ripping through more waves before ripping along street corners, colliding with corpses, sending them hurtling toward brick walls and through shop windows.

"WHAT'S YOUR PLAN?" shouted Jeremiah as he put the final wrappings on Fantasia's neck, then carefully securing her into her seat.

"I HAVE NO IDEA! I'VE SEEN CRAZY SHIT IN MY DAY, BUT THIS!...HOLD ON!"

I weaved around another corner, planning to circle the block. The main road in town ran from east to west, upon our first exit, we went west, the only chance we had left was going in the opposite direction. I tossed a gun to Jeremiah as I jerked the wheel hard, sending the truck spinning around another corner.

"KEEP THEM OFF OUR TAIL!" I shouted, pointing at the bed of the truck.

The undead showed their stamina and strength with their reactions to the trucks blows. At this point, instead of being thrown away from the truck, they had begun clutching the sides and working their way into the bed of the truck, then towards the back window. I heard the shatter of the glass as Jeremiah smashed out the back window, then began firing at them repeatedly, sending their torso's ragged, and with each bump, another was launched out of the truck. With a few more sharp turns, the truck had positioned itself in the direction that we needed to go, and I slammed a foot down heavily on the gas pedal, with no intention of slowing down. 80, 100, 120, 140, 160, 180 mph. The truck let out a fierce roar as we ripped down the road, approaching the sign stating "Now Leaving Smithland." I gritted my teeth at the feeling of a sharp pain in my gut. It was one of warning. Something telling me that something was very wrong. Something horrible, and with that, I screamed to everyone's full attention.

"DAMN IT, HOLD ON!!!!" The truck rammed into a line of invisibility, marking the barrier of the town.

The truck rolled several times, and as we rolled, my mind continuously slipped back and forth between thoughts of death and what had happened. I couldn't help but focus my eyes back toward the road, trying to find the barrier we had rammed into, but there was nothing. It seemed the only thing blocking the road was a wall of cement-like air. The truck rolled to a stop on it's roof. My body flopping back into the seat, ragged. My neck snapped grotesquely as I stared at the others throughout the truck. Jeremiah hung lifeless from his seatbelt, as did Dave.

Fantasia was no where to be seen. My heart sank. She must have been launched out of the window! I started to sob, then directed my attention back towards town. The army was approaching. I fumbled for my knife and cut my way through my seat belt, landing on layers of broken medal and shattered glass with a thud. I let out a dull yelp, then drug myself out of the window. I used the side of the truck to drag myself to my feet, and could feel my limbs snap as I drew my gun from it's holster. I began picking off as many as possible, sending each of them tumbling in a cloud of dirt, but only managed to get through seven before they reached me. They launched through the air similar to a cheetah attacking it's prey, sending me crashing to the ground, and began ripping at my flesh with their teeth, I screamed once more, until I felt it fading away with my life, as I watched my horribly obscene vision fade to darkness.

The End

I woke up with a groan. An intense pain shot through my body as I sat up. In my hand I held a foreign object, which I could not make out until my vision had snapped back. It was Smiles, the puppet. My eyes shot around the area, looking for answers to what had happened. Beside me lay Jeremiah, Dave, and Fantasia, who had all woken up with the same pain fueled groans.

"What the hell happened?" I questioned, running my hand over my forehead.

"Look", instructed Jeremiah, pointing at a road sign perched just beyond us.

It read "Smithland, 30 miles". We each climbed to our feet, slowly, trying to force out a smile, but our ability being eliminated by the intense pain that echoed throughout our bodies. Once standing, I made my way to Fantasia, helping her off the ground, and helping her stand with one arm over my shoulder.

"Are we....free?", she asked, speaking with a weak tone.

"Yeah....We're finally free...And We'll never have to come back, babe."

"What'll we do now?", questioned Jeremiah, who was still crouched on one knee, but staring up at me with a worn face.

I stared at each of my new family members, and then looked back at Smiles, who I still clutched into my hand, waiting for his always helpful suggestions. With only a moments hesitation, I had my answer. I rose my attention back towards the group, and announced.

"Now... Now we kill." With that, we set off down the road, making our way to the next town, leaving the burning remains of Smithland in the distance.

Made in the USA
Monee, IL
01 April 2021